RIM OF THE RANGE

Johnny Malcolm, foreman of the Wagon Wheel, had a problem. His boss was considering turning the ranch over to sheep, and had left the decision to Johnny. 'Sheep' was a dirty word as far as Johnny was concerned, and would also mean trouble with the neighboring Axe range. But before Johnny could make up his mind, a bullet almost made it up for him—and led him to a shack where destiny awaited...

RIM OF THE RANGE

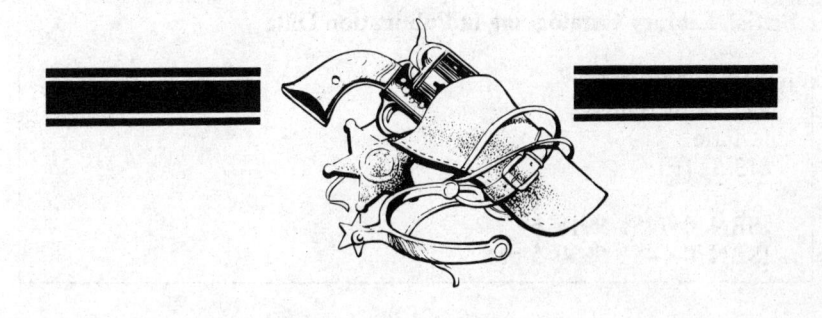

Archie Joscelyn

ATLANTIC LARGE PRINT
Chivers Press, Bath, England.
Curley Publishing, Inc.,
South Yarmouth, Mass., USA.

Library of Congress Cataloging-in-Publication Data

Joscelyn, Archie, 1899–
  Rim of the range / Archie Joscelyn.
    p. cm.—(Atlantic large print)
  ISBN 0–7927–0367–7 (softcover)
  1. Large type books. I. Title.
[PS3519.O712R48 1990]
813'.52—dc20   90-37703
                                                           CIP

British Library Cataloguing in Publication Data

Joscelyn, Archie *1899–*
  Rim of the range.
  I. Title
  813.52 [F]

  ISBN 0–7451–9918–6
  ISBN 0–7451–9930–5 pbk

This Large Print edition is published by Chivers Press, England, and Curley Publishing, Inc, U.S.A. 1990

Published by arrangement with Donald MacCampbell, Inc

U.K. Hardback   ISBN 0 7451 9918 6
U.K. Softback   ISBN 0 7451 9930 5
U.S.A. Softback ISBN 0 7927 0367 7

© Copyright 1963, by Arcadia House

*For Ruby and Gordon Montgomery
In memory of many kindnesses*

RIM OF THE RANGE

CHAPTER ONE

Rain swept in gusts out of a sagebrush-tinted sky, driven by a prankish wind. John Malcolm's long jaws were coldly bedewed, his lean frame shivering, despite his slicker. May was a spring month, but in Wyoming it could be rawly dank. In a larger sense, the weather was like that part of the country—beguiling, full of promise. But somehow the promise was never quite fulfilled.

For the past ten days, the crew of Wagon Wheel had been busy with roundup. During all that period the clouds had lowered, promising rain.

Rainfall had been insufficient every year since Malcolm had come to that range a decade before. He had grown from scraggly youth to lean-fleshed manhood, but the land's promise remained unfulfilled. Instead of springing rich and full-bodied, the grass curled thin and sparse, and the rains which might have made the difference between leanness and prosperity stopped short at the Big Horn, a day's ride to the west.

If additional proof was needed, the roundup had furnished it. Howard Denning, turning as grizzled as summer grass, was a cattleman by instinct as well as by training; with all the range which was at his disposal, the Wagon Wheel should have been rolling as on a downhill grade. Instead, it was a hard scrabble, and its groanings and squealings could almost be heard. The calf crop of the ranch was always short, the winter loss heavier than could be borne. It was demanding country, giving little in return. It was necessary to run at full speed to make sure merely of standing still; even with prodigious effort, there was always danger of losing ground.

After ten rainy days, the top soil was scarcely wet enough to look muddy. It was drizzle, Oregon mist; never a soaker. And this year, the lack of good spring rains could spell the difference between the Wheel keeping turning and being broken and discarded.

Smoke lifted in a discouraged twist from the chimney of the cook house, whipped back upon itself by the blustering wind. He was late for the first under-cover meal in nearly two weeks. As Malcolm stabled his horse, the disconsolate lowing of the herd drifted from the corrals. On Denning's order, they had held all the gather—calves, cows, yearlings, prime beef. The herd was behind bars, instead of being permitted to race back to the range, as was customary, once the branding was finished. Their voices mourned in never-ending protest.

Denning had not explained the order, even

to his foreman. He had always made his own decisions and kept his own counsel. Johnny pushed open the door, shaking his slicker. The crew were at the table, most of them looking as rough as a steer in March. Three or four who had found the opportunity to shave looked out of place. The savory odors of food wafted from the stove. Bowls of stew were along the big table, while a pudding cooled on the stove's high oven.

The men looked up at the foreman's approach and went on eating. Howard Denning nodded. It struck Johnny anew how grizzled he had become, the rawhiding effect of a year of strain. Denning was big, troubled by an old injury to his left leg which gave a list to his walk. Once in the saddle, he was as good as ever, but getting on and off a horse was a painful chore. For the past year, he'd done less and less riding, leaving the responsibility in Johnny's hands.

Johnny slid into his own place, accepted the bowl of stew which Cy Robbins shoved toward him, helped himself from a heaped platter of biscuits, and downed a scalding cup of coffee. He could feel its bite all the way down. It helped dispel the numbness, and he ate silently, catching up with the others. Hungry men had no time for talk. Only when Dinty Toole, his red face matching his stubble of beard, started to scrape back from the table did Denning's heavy bass check him.

'I'd like for everybody to stay,' he requested. 'I've a word for the ears of every man.'

Dinty looked surprised, a quick glint coming and going in his eyes. Johnny had seen the same sort of look in the eyes of a trapped coyote, watching a rifle muzzle center on it. It lasted only an instant; then Dinty reached for another biscuit.

Howard Denning placed both hands on the table, shoving his bulk partially back but not rising. This was the second time in ten years that he'd made any general announcement to the whole crew. The last previous occasion had been seven years before, when he'd informed them that twenty-year-old Johnny Malcolm was their new foreman.

'I've something to say that you may not like,' Denning began, and the muscles of his face knotted. 'And the devil of it is, I don't much like it myself. But hear me out, and afterward each of you can make up your minds as to what you wish to do. Whatever you decide, there should be no hard feelings.'

They eyed him expectantly, intrigued. His face again twisted in what might have been a rueful smile. Then, blunt as always, he gave it to them without preamble.

'I'm going into the sheep business.'

They stared, doubting the evidence of their ears, looking at one another and back at him.

Had he suggested that he'd found a trail to purgatory, with good grass somewhere along the way, and wanted them to take the herd there, they would have accepted the statement and the request without question. But this was beyond belief.

'You heard me right,' Denning grunted. 'I'm quitting cattle and going into the business of raising sheep. I know how you feel,' he went on. 'So do I. I've been born and raised a cattleman, and cattlemen hate sheep and sheepmen. I know all the arguments: the stink of sheep, their eternal bleating that can drive a man crazy, the way they eat grass into the roots and destroy a range, the fact that cattle won't graze where sheep have run. If anyone had suggested to me, even half a year ago, that I'd ever turn sheepman myself, I'd have called him crazy—and probably worse.

'But lately I've been doing a lot of thinking, and I've made up my mind that hanging onto pride and cattle and going deeper broke each year is the way of a fool, especially when there's a good chance that with sheep I can make the sort of money I've got to have. So I'm choosing sheep.'

He looked about, half-challengingly, half-hopefully. The first shock vanished from most faces, leaving only a careful blankness. Johnny swallowed his last spoonful of pudding, realizing that though it was his favorite, he hadn't tasted the other mouthfuls. He was beginning to understand. Money. It sounded crass and materialistic, but Howard had an excellent reason for wanting to make money.

A year before, Ma Denning had been hurt when a team had run away, spilling Ma onto the icy ground. At first, turning a grimace into a grin as they lifted her, she'd kidded them if not herself. Her injury hadn't seemed to amount to much. They'd gotten her to town and the doctor, making her as comfortable as possible, padding the wagon box with hay and blankets. Everyone, including the doctor, had figured that she'd be back in her own kitchen within a matter of ten days or two weeks, as good as ever.

Instead, six weeks later, she had made the hundred-mile journey to the railroad, thence to St. Paul and a bevy of specialists. She had written back that they clustered around her like chicks around an old hen. Something was wrong, a twist and a hidden injury.

Now, a year later, Ma was still in St. Paul, still undergoing treatment and operations, with the result still in doubt.

The one thing about which there was no doubt was the cost. The next operation which was to be tried would be very costly. Howard Denning had told the doctors to go ahead, but Johnny had wondered privately where the money was coming from. This time, Howard couldn't afford to go to St. Paul. He'd made the trip twice. He went on, his voice flat.

'I made the same mistake, coming in here, a lot of others have—I supposed this was cattle country. It's not. What do we have? Broken range, gullies and a few small hills. A lot of brush and sagebrush, a scattering of scrub trees. The hills to the west of us are too far away to do us any good as winter shelter. The rains stop at those same hills. Here they keep tantalizing us with the promise of plenty of rain, but what do we get? In ten days of riding, we've been damp all the while but never once wet!'

That was true. This was the rim of good rangeland.

'With plenty of range, I figured to make it, but other factors are against cattle. The grass grows scant and thin, so that the cows are never quite in condition. The calf crop is always short, and those who live out the summer are never in good shape to stand the winter. Our losses run too high. Our beef, when we market it, is far from prime—it's a long drive to the railroad, and shrinkage all the way to Chicago. In short, it's a losing game, because this is not cattle country.

'With sheep, it should be a different story. They can graze and grow fat where cattle will all but starve. They spend the nights in corrals, because of coyotes and wolves, and those corrals can be roofed, as they often are for sheep. So in the cold of winter sheep lie snug. And when a crop of wool is harvested, there's no shrinkage in a long drive to market.

'So I figure this is sheep range, and I am driving every last head of stock to the railroad, shipping east to Chicago, and selling. Most of the money will pay for nine thousand head of sheep, for which I have already more or less contracted. They will be shipped back by the railroad, then driven here. Since there is a bridge across the Termagent, it should work fine.'

The Termagent was a tributary of the Big Horn River, lying a third of the way to the railroad, athwart their path. In bygone years its high banks and swift waters had posed an ugly problem, only partially solved by a ferry. Now it had been bridged.

Howard's glance roved questioningly. There was no comment, and he went on.

'I may lose my shirt, but it's too ragged to matter much. Of course, my neighbors will hate me for bringing sheep to this range. There will be trouble. But it is my land, and I have made up my mind. If you prefer not to work for a sheepman, there will be no hard feelings on my part. If some of you decide to stay, I'll like that. Think it over and let me know.'

CHAPTER TWO

This time, Denning shoved clear back from the table, balancing himself heavily as he stood up. His glance fixed on Malcolm, as did the others' eyes. He knew, as did Johnny, that most if not all of the crew would follow his lead.

That was not entirely because he was the foreman, the man from whom they were accustomed to take orders. They respected the boss, and they loved Ma Denning and wished her well. But Howard Denning was a hard man, taciturn and aloof, though a good employer. It was to the foreman that they instinctively turned. He'd been Johnny to everyone before becoming foreman, and while they still called him that, it was with respect.

He had an easy smile and a competence which seemed equally unforced. He had been a natural choice for foreman, even though most of the crew had been his seniors. Not only did he know cattle and how to handle them, but he possessed qualities of leadership. In war he would have been a general. Where he led, others followed unquestioningly, even gladly.

He drew a deep breath and gave a partial answer.

'What you say makes sense, Howard. One thing sure: this ain't cattle country. I hadn't considered the other, but it might be good range for sheep. As you say, that's a gamble. As for the other part—well, this is sort of sudden. I'll want to think it over before deciding.'

'That's what I want you to do, all of you,' Denning agreed. 'I wouldn't want anyone to stay who didn't feel right about it. On the other hand—' He drew a deep breath and made a surprising confession. 'I reckon Ma would like it better, when she gets home, to find the boys she knows still underfoot.'

Johnny doubted if that was what he had started to say, but it was hard for Howard to express himself, particularly on emotional or personal matters. In any case, he had hit the right note. They'd do more for Ma than for anyone else on earth. And that was as it should be.

On the other hand, there was a deep, virtually unbridgeable gulf between sheepmen and cattlemen. Cowboys, raised in the tradition, found even the suggestion of sheep shocking. This had been cattle country, with no sheep anywhere. Whoever broke the unwritten law and was the first to deviate from the standard, bringing sheep to the range, would find himself ostracized, hated, bitterly opposed by former friends and neighbors.

Few, if any, could be expected to understand. Even if they did, they probably would not accept or forgive. If Denning's crew stuck with him, they could count on suffering from the same hatred, which would almost certainly erupt into violence. Sheep would never be permitted on the range without a fight.

'I think maybe a few head of cows are still ranging back toward Lampases Spring,' Johnny observed. 'I've been aiming to ride and have a look.'

'Sure,' Denning agreed understandingly. Johnny could just as well have sent a man, but he wanted time to think.

Selecting a fresh horse, Johnny saddled it, then made a small pack, since he might well be gone overnight. There was still a tantalizing beat of rain in his face as he headed west by north. The lowering clouds looked as though they might spill a deluge at any moment, but they had had that look for weeks.

He pondered as he rode, not at all certain what his decision would be. Had it not been for Ma Denning, there would have been no question. As a cowboy, foreman for a big outfit, thereby virtually on a footing with the cattlemen, he would have remained loyal to the tradition, riding to hunt a new job, doing so without qualms. Howard Denning was a tough man, giving few favors and asking less.

He'd make out.

But Ma was different. She had been Ma to every one of them. And now she was flat on her back, among strangers, with less than a fifty-fifty chance that she'd ever walk again, or even return to the land she loved so well.

Johnny pushed steadily but without hurry. He saw no fresh sign of the cattle he'd believed might be hiding off that way.

He saw something else which caused him to wonder: a wheel trace, showing at intervals where conditions were right, lost again where the ground had been hard or the grass had grown well.

That was odd. As a foreman, he knew pretty well what occurred on Wagon Wheel range, as well as in the surrounding country. But he, like others of the crew, didn't venture that far back very often, and he'd had no word from anyone of such a wagon. Certainly it didn't belong to the ranch. And who else would come there with a wagon, or why?

Probably it wasn't important, but he was intrigued.

In late afternoon the clouds broke, allowing the sun to pour through in brief glory. This was his first glimpse of the sun in three days, and welcome.

It was as the sun came out that he saw the other track—this the hoofprints of a shod horse, much fresher than the wagon wheel trace. The hoofmark was only days old, and something about it intrigued him. It might have been made by one of his own crew on roundup, but he doubted that. Just over a low hill he found it again, and his hunch was confirmed.

Here the rider had halted, dismounting to rest and look about, to build and smoke a quirly. Part of the sodden remains of the cigarette attested to that. His horse had cropped the grass, making a small, hungry circle, as though held by an impatient rein and forced to eat around the bit.

There was something else. The ground had been fairly soft from the rain, but on that part of the knoll it was normally quite solid, and where the man had stood, little grass ever grew. The marks of high heels were deep, clearly imprinted, as though he had moved impatiently.

There was nothing unusual about that. Cowboys all wore high-heeled boots. But few cowboys wore boots as distinctive as these. In three separate imprints, Johnny found the insignia which subsequent rain had not quite dissolved. A sign like a brand—which was, in fact, a brand. The Axe.

Barney Vascom's Broken Axe was the other big outfit in that part of the country. A proud, arrogant man, Barney Vascom carried his personal foibles to the point of special footwear for himself and his relatives. His boots, and the boots of his son, his nephew and his daughter were hand-made. And in the bottom of the high heels was a replica of the brand of his outfit, the broken shaft of the axe handle, with the axe head attached.

One of those four had ridden there only a few days before on Wagon Wheel range. It was not a woman's boot, so it must have been one of the three men.

There was another oddity. Despite the shoe being hand-made, the brand being cut deep into the heel, the boot was beginning to be run down at heel and toe.

The sign was days old; certainly there was no reason for apprehension, but he looked about sharply before riding on. Some things were sure in an uncertain world. And the surest was that Barney Vascom and the Broken Axe would most violently oppose Howard Denning bringing sheep to the range.

There had always been bad blood between the two outfits, and though a sort of truce had existed for some time, the mere mention of sheep would be enough to break it. But the news of Denning's intention was still a secret from all save his own crew.

Johnny had found no sign of the cattle he sought, nor was he likely to now. There was a small spring bubbling from under a mossy boulder at the edge of a clump of cottonwoods. This was Lampases Spring, the only one which did not go dry by midsummer. Johnny unsaddled, picketed his horse and built a small fire, finding dry wood without much difficulty, further proof of how scanty the rain had been.

He delved among his provisions, bringing out some cold biscuits, preparing to fry bacon and boil coffee. He was tired from the long strain of roundup, looking forward to relaxing and a long lazy evening. With that in mind he'd brought along a special treat: a can of condensed milk for his coffee—ninety-nine times in a hundred he drank it black—and cans of tomatoes. He had hoped for peaches, but the cook had grumpily informed him that none were in the larder.

The sun was gone now, the last of its glory painting the west. The coffee started to boil over. He leaned, reaching quickly to grab and move it back, and the movement saved his life. A bullet tore a small hole in the near side of the coffeepot, a gaping tear in the far side as it exploded through the liquid, scattering it over the blaze. The shock almost jerked the pot from his hand, and an instant later, as he threw himself flat, he heard the jarring note of a rifle from some distance off at one side.

CHAPTER THREE

Johnny's action, in jerking back and flattening himself was instinctive. He lay without moving. The spilled coffee had put out the fire, leaving sudden darkness where before had been a revealing patch of light.

The bullet would certainly have buried itself near his heart but for his sudden movement. Now his action, as though he had jerked at the impact of a bullet and fallen, might deceive the rifleman into believing that his aim had been good. It was a hunch worth playing.

The shot had come from a considerable distance. There was nothing to see. Johnny reached for his revolver, then waited, ears alert, since eyes were of scant use.

Nothing happened. Either the gunman was satisfied that his shot had accomplished the desired result, or else he was too canny to investigate and perhaps stop a bullet in turn. When it became reasonably certain that no one was coming, Johnny quietly gathered up his duffel and rode a mile to the side before camping again. He did not risk another fire.

The clouds thickened again, and there were more spatters of rain. Sometime after midnight the sky cleared. He awoke to bright sunshine and a sharp chill, with frost everywhere.

He was reasonably certain that the killer would not have remained close at hand. A man who shot in such fashion, without warning, then exhibited such caution, would be discreet enough to remove well away during the hours of darkness.

Nonetheless, Johnny chose a likely spot, where it was possible to watch on all sides, before cooking breakfast. He opened a tin of tomatoes, eating them, then used the can to boil coffee in. He did not bother with the frills which he had originally planned. Afterward, he rode to where he estimated the shot might have come from, and the slight rain was his ally. He found the tracks of the same horse which he had encountered earlier. Nearby, the gunman had stretched in the grass and taken careful aim; only the sudden boiling over of the coffee had spoiled the shot. A heel print, with the blurred brand of the Axe, was a final confirmation.

The killer might still be prowling, with no compunctions against further attacks from ambush. The word concerning sheep had not yet been spread abroad, so it must be something else which had caused one of the members of the Vascom clan to have a try at murder. It might have been no more than long-smoldering animosity and a perfect opportunity. But it would bear looking into.

The sun was beginning to wipe off the

frost, but enough remained to show that no horseman had ridden thereabouts since before dawn. Half a mile farther on, Johnny found another trace of the wagon, the sign as old as before. Then, among a small jumble of gullies and low hills, he came upon the wagon itself.

It was an ancient vehicle, its paint long since peeled—almost as though it had been retrieved from the discard. It was almost hidden behind a clump of brush. A stone's throw from it was a cabin, almost equally weathered, so well concealed by its surroundings that Johnny had never suspected its existence. It must have stood deserted and forgotten for many years.

He rode cautiously nearer, maintaining a sharp lookout. A magpie squawked from a tree and flapped away at his approach, and that seemed a fair indication that no one else was lurking. Nonetheless, remembering the closeness of that rifle bullet, the venom behind it, he left his horse among trees and brush and proceeded on foot.

He could see no fresh sign since the rain, but there was older evidence of occupancy. Someone had gone in and out of the door several times. There was the beginning of a path, leading to a spring at the edge of the gulch. Slop water had been thrown out from the door, enough to leave its own sign.

A rusty length of stovepipe protruded from the roof. He was about to hail when a noise startled him—the last sound he had ever expected to hear, under such conditions or in such a place.

It was the hungry, fretful wailing of a baby.

The complaint was not loud. It was as though the child were too weak or tired to put much effort even into crying, a despairing, lonely plaint.

Johnny listened, incredulous, but there could be no mistake. The wail came from inside the house. There was no other sound. He went to the door, hesitated briefly and knocked.

The wailing stopped. There was no answer. Half-consciously he noted that the door was still solid and substantial. It dragged a little as he pushed, but it had recently been rehung on rusty iron hinges, replacing leather ones, the remnants of which still showed.

Even with such a warning he was not prepared for what he saw. The old shack had been erected long years before and had apparently stood abandoned for most of them. It had never amounted to much, nor had its furnishings.

There was an ancient rickety table, made of boards, perched on uncertain legs. A couple of bunks were on one wall. There was an old stool, a box nailed up to serve as a cupboard, a combined cooking and heating stove. It stood in a corner, one side propped up with a stone, barely usable.

There was one extra piece of furniture. It was a small trunk, brass-bound, the lid standing open. Inside, upon a mattress of blankets, covered by others, lay the baby.

A woman was in the lower bunk, looking at him with great, hopefully expectant eyes. Her face looked doubly pale in contrast with the rich, almost scarlet red of her hair, now in disarray about her head.

Johnny crossed the room, staring down with a sense of shock. It was half a year since he'd seen the girl, perhaps more. He remembered her as a bright-eyed, laughing person, shy, with a wild, strange beauty, enhanced by the richness of her hair, a witchery which lurked in her eyes. It was Myra, the daughter of Old Man M'Ginnis, who had a small spread of his own just out of town. At least he'd had it until a short time ago, when he'd died—some said of a broken heart.

That was hard to believe of so hard-shelled a man, but it might be true. He'd been harsh and overly protective of his daughter, perhaps because he loved her but hardly knew how to care for a girl-child. Nearly a year before, she had run away to town and had taken a job in the Mercantile, clerking, against her father's wishes. Report had it that he'd ordered her to return home, then, strangely humble, had begged her to come back.

She did not have red hair for nothing. She

had refused to return. Like most of the men on the range, Johnny had found excuses to drop into the Mercantile oftener than business really required, more frequently than in the days before Myra had gone to work there. She had been friendly with him, as with others, but never more than that. It hadn't taken long to understand why.

She was deeply infatuated with Leavitt Vascom, the worthless nephew of Old Barney.

Johnny had liked her, even as he'd felt sorry for her. Old Man M'Ginnis had warned the Vascoms that he'd empty a double-barreled shotgun, loaded with buckshot, into any one of them who dared set foot on his land. That, probably, had been the reason Myra had left home and refused to return. A woman in love could see no evil in the object of her affections.

Later, both she and Leavitt Vascom had disappeared. It had been rumored that they had eloped. And M'Ginnis had died—perhaps of a broken heart.

And it was to this that Leavitt had brought her! Johnny saw her lips move and bent lower. Her voice was hardly more than a whisper.

'John! Thank heaven you've come!'

He dropped on his knees, filled with a sense of outrage, also a feeling of helplessness.

'Myra! What's happened?'

'Could you get me a drink?' she asked. 'And the baby—it's starving. If somehow you could feed it—the poor little thing—'

'I'll get you some water,' he promised. 'And I'll try to do something for the baby,' he added desperately. There was an old battered bucket under the table. Questions could wait. He snatched up the pail and hurried to the spring, filled the bucket and returned. He found a cup in the cupboard and held the water to her lips, raising her gently with one hand behind her back, shocked anew at how very thin and wasted she was. She drank slowly, swallowing with difficulty, but her eyes expressed her gratitude as she sank back.

'Thanks, John,' she breathed. 'That was good. You were always good—always kind—'

She broke off, coughing, and if he had not already known it, he would have been sure that she was desperately ill. 'How long since you've had anything to eat?' he demanded.

'I don't know.' She seemed to consider. 'I can't remember. That doesn't matter now. I'm not even hungry any more. But the baby—she must be starving.'

He nodded and went out again. For the next few minutes he worked with a sort of repressed desperation, gathering wood, building a fire in the stove. The baby had stopped crying, settling down to a sort of discouraged murmuring and muttering, and as he drew back a corner of the blanket he saw that she was trying to suck her own fist. She was tiny and red, somewhat like a kitten, and he was appalled but determined.

He heated water in a battered kettle, emptying another can of tomatoes into it, along with chunks of bacon. It would make a soup in the least possible time, not too strong, yet reasonably nourishing. He found the can of condensed milk, thankful now that it had gone unopened. After rinsing the tomato can, he poured some milk into it, diluting it with water, and warmed it. That would be the best he could contrive for the baby.

But how should he feed it to her? He saw a small, empty bottle among the few articles which passed for dishes and household utensils in the makeshift cupboard. He washed it with hot water, pondering, then hurried to his duffel bag again. He brought out a new, unused pair of fancy riding gloves, sliced off one finger, cut a small hole in the end, and pulled it over the neck of the bottle. It was makeshift, but the best he could manage.

The baby was fretting again, crying, a wail of hunger and despair. He picked her up, blanket and all. He noted how wet it was, but for the moment there was no time to think of that. Clumsily he cradled her in one arm, holding the bottle with the other, thrusting the nipple into her mouth.

Her wail rose louder, then subsided, and all at once, as some of the warm milk ran into her mouth, she began eating hungrily. She choked a few times, by which he guessed that it flowed too freely, but by tipping it back, drawing fresh wails of outrage, he managed fairly well. She ate with a sort of starving desperation, and her eyes, very blue, came open and fixed on his face. She seemed to be considering him, deciding that perhaps he was not too bad, after all. He caught a glimpse of Myra's face and saw that she was watching, tender approval in her eyes.

The baby choked; then he saw that the bottle was empty. It didn't seem much, but perhaps it was enough for so small a person, especially when she had been without food. He saw her eyes close and placed her gently back in the trunk. At least she would be in somewhat better shape for a while, and he felt a strange glow of pride that he had been able to cope with so unexpected a situation.

'I'll fix some soup for you now,' he promised, turning to Myra. 'Then you'll feel better, too.'

To his surprise, she shook her head.

'Thanks, but don't bother,' she whispered. 'It's too late—for that. And I want to talk—while there's time. Sit down, please.'

He hesitated, then obeyed mutely, suddenly afraid of what he saw in her face. He took one thin hand in both of his.

'Myra, Myra, what has happened to you?' he asked. 'Is Leavitt responsible for this?'

She nodded, her eyes dark and tragic.

'I should have listened to you—or to Papa,' she said wanly. 'I didn't understand then that you both wanted what was best for me. I thought Leavitt loved me. I loved him.'

'You poor kid.'

'I guess you can't help such things.' She sighed. 'I only found out—after it was too late—that he thought Pa had a lot of money, and that he'd get hold of it. When Pa died, and he found that all he had was a mortgage, he—he came back here, and he was terrible!'

'And you—with the baby?' Johnny asked sternly.

'Not then. That was two or three weeks ago, at least as nearly as I can tell. The baby was born a few days ago—two or three, I think. I don't remember very well.'

'You mean that you were all alone?' he asked incredulously.

'I managed—somehow,' she said. 'But I'm dying, Johnny. I've been sick—awfully sick—for weeks. It doesn't matter—I guess it's better this way. But the baby deserves a chance. She isn't responsible for any of what I did, or him.'

'No,' he agreed, 'she isn't. I'll try and see that she gets a chance. But—do you mean that he went off and left you—knowing what was going to happen—went away when you were so ill?'

'I think he only came back to see if I was dead already,' she said resignedly. 'When he found out that there was no money and would be none, he was furious, and I was only in the way. He taunted me that I wasn't even his wife—that the marriage ceremony had been a mockery, a fake. But I thought it was real, Johnny. I'd never have gone with him if I hadn't!'

'I'm sure you wouldn't,' Johnny agreed. 'The striped cousin to a civet!' he added under his breath. 'The low-down crawlin' sidewinder!'

He checked and started, realizing suddenly that she was no longer listening. Bending closer, he felt cold. Somehow, in the face of sickness, weakness and starvation, she had willed to keep alive until someone should come. She had done it for love of her baby, enduring until she had whispered her story in a few stark words, making sure that he would look after the child. Now there had been nothing more to keep her.

From where he had left it, partially hidden, his horse neighed, which probably meant that it had heard or scented another horse approaching. Under the circumstances, that would almost certainly be Leavitt Vascom, prowling with uneasy fear as a spur. The bullet, fired to stop him short of the cabin the evening before, was now understandable.

CHAPTER FOUR

As Johnny stepped to the door, the horseman came into sight, riding not up but down the gulch, appearing around the screening leaves of a clump of chokecherries, white with bloom. Like all the Vascoms, he rode a high-stepping horse, a blooded animal imported from Kentucky. Not for the Vascoms were the half-wild descendants of the Indian ponies, the tireless cayuses such as the one Johnny had ridden. Old Barney Vascom had a high and bitter pride, astringent as iodine. In everything he had to have the best.

Leavitt Vascom had fared better than he deserved because of that pride of his uncle's. Half a dozen times in as many years he had strayed from the home range, a fiddle-footed man intent on making his own way with the power of his fists and his gun. Each time he had returned, sometimes no more than a jump ahead of the law, seeking sanctuary and finding it. Barney's anger had been bitter and raw, his disgust vented in fleering words, but because Leavitt was his brother's son, Barney had stood with him against all outsiders.

Some men learn their lesson from adversity, but Leavitt was not one of those. The same high arrogance was in his darkly handsome face, untempered by contrition or remorse or any doubt of himself. He was solid as well as tall, as powerfully built as Old Barney, lacking only the ruggedness in the face of adversity. His horse had been coming at a trot, as though eagerness were tempered by caution. Now, seeing Johnny, rage seemed to explode in Vascom's face, and he struck savagely with the spurs, sending the blooded animal into a wild gallop.

He pulled it up with a vicious bit, just abreast of Johnny, and sat staring down, his dark eyes almost opaque, his too heavy chin jutting beneath the trimmed elegance of a brown mustache.

'What the devil are you doing here, you stinkin' sheepherder?' he challenged.

Johnny heard the epithet with a sense of shock. Sheepherder!

It was only the day before that Howard Denning had revealed his plans and intention to his own crew. Yet already the word had spread, and that indicated more than a loose tongue in a blabbermouth. For the news to have reached this scion of the Vascoms so swiftly, there must be a traitor in Wagon Wheel's crew, one who also drew pay from the rival Axe.

Johnny returned the stare. His lip twisted in contempt.

'What do you think?' he asked. 'This is Wagon Wheel range. Who invited *you* here?'

A flicker of Vascom's eyes suggested that he had forgotten that it was he who was trespassing, but to him that meant little. His voice was a snarl.

'You would have to come sneaking, spying—sticking your snout in where it doesn't belong—'

'Meaning Myra?' Johnny demanded. 'I suppose you came back to bury her, figuring she'd surely be dead by now, wanting to cover all trace of your own treachery! Oh, I know how you pretended to marry her, but cheated even on that, then had to hide it, for you knew that your uncle wouldn't stand for the double-crossing deal you had in mind. Even he can't stomach some of your actions. So you got her off here and kept her out of sight, and when you found that Old M'Ginnis didn't have any money, you told her she wasn't really your wife, and left her when you knew she was dying!'

Leavitt grew quiet as he spoke, listening, his face momentarily like the grass at dawn. Abruptly he dropped the reins and swung down from the saddle, and Johnny recognized the signs. Report had it that Leavitt had killed three or four men, not always in fair fight. With the bluster gone, he was dangerous.

'Dead, is she?' he asked. 'It's about time. She's been long enough doing it.' The callousness of his words was even more shocking than what Johnny had seen. 'I'll admit I was fooled. I thought M'Ginnis had a lot of loot stashed away, and money is for spending. But I guess I got even with him—taking his chick away. They say it killed him, and good riddance. As for her—she was in my way. I've other and bigger plans, and couldn't be bothered.'

Deliberately, he unbuckled his gun belt and tossed it to one side. His smile was mocking.

'I'm just as bad as you figured, ain't I—all the bad Vascom blood, along with the Slade, coming to a head! But I make no bones about it. Your sort are mealy-mouthed hypocrites, who pretend in public and are devils in private. I never could stomach that sort of double-dealing. I could beat you with a gun, but I prefer to kill you with my hands. *If you've got the guts to fight back! If not—*' His shrug was eloquent.

The monstrous conceit of the man was amazing. He could convince himself that what he wanted was right, that what he said was true, even while knowing that with guns he would be helpless before the greater speed and accuracy of John Malcolm's Colts. So he tossed aside the gun, to compel Johnny to meet him on his own terms, where he expected to possess the advantage. He was fully as tall, his reach as long. And in weight, Johnny would have to give him a full forty pounds.

It was foolish to accept such a taunt, to allow a man who boasted that he had no scruples to dictate the terms. But pride was in Malcolm, as high a pride as a Vascom might boast, and his anger was at the bursting point. He unbuckled his own gun belt and tossed it to the side while Leavitt waited, a smile twisting his mouth unpleasantly.

'You're a fool,' he said. 'And I'm going to kill you.'

He rushed, not hitting, his long arms reaching out. Johnny side-stepped, then evaded a murderous twisting kick, in which the long-shanked spur at boot's end was set to slash down his belly. He had never seen so sharp-toothed a spur, and there was blood on the wheel.

The raking kick came close. It spoiled his own timing, so that his plan to catch Vascom's jaw with his own fist nearly failed. His knuckles slid along the bulge of the chin. Before he could recover, Leavitt attained his objective. His arms closed around Johnny, jerking Johnny against him savagely, while at the same time, exerting all his strength, Leavitt threw him to the ground and came down on top.

The shock of the fall, with two hundred and ten pounds crashing above him, almost knocked the breath from Malcolm's body. But Johnny had the stamina of the longhorn which had battled a variety of enemies and survived heavy odds. The memory of Myra, of the appeal she had made, and the baby, asleep now inside the cabin, gave him strength. If he failed, more than himself would die.

Then, for the first time, he felt a pang of fear and grabbed desperately, forcing a half-numbed arm to do his will. The full, calculated treachery of Leavitt was apparent in that moment.

It had seemed on the surface almost a magnanimous gesture to rid himself of his gun, toss it away, offer a fair fight, fist to fists, man to man. But that had been no part of Vascom's plan. The odds might favor Leavitt in such a contest, but they were not sure enough. He'd had more in mind, and now it gleamed in his hand—a long-bladed bowie, produced from a hidden sheath, the glittering, needle-pointed dagger only inches above Johnny's throat.

Vascom's weight pinned him down. It was impossible to throw him off or to twist out from under. Vascom's left hand was on his right wrist, pinning it to the ground. Only with his left hand could Johnny fight the right arm which held the blade, and again the contest was unequal, all the odds in favor of the dagger.

Leavitt was panting, as much from rage as from exertion. Johnny felt his muscles crack and buckle with strain. The eyes above glared into his, hot with triumph. The point of the blade was reaching, descending, despite Johnny's desperate efforts to hold it back. Somewhere at the side, Vascom's horse snorted, as though it sniffed the odor of death.

Johnny knew how it would be, and in one way it would be good. When death came, it would be mercifully swift. He couldn't hold the knife away much longer. His muscles would give way eventually, for the greater weight was overwhelming. Right arm against left, when both men were right-handed, was in itself a tremendous advantage for Vascom.

Leavitt was triumphant, completely sure of himself and the outcome. As nearly as Johnny had been able to gather, Myra had lived, hidden away in there, for more than half a year, and in all that time, he was the first outsider to venture close or find the cabin. Vascom had no fear that anyone else would happen along to interfere or offer help, or to discover his crime, once it was covered with several feet of earth.

A sound startled both of them—the cry of the baby, from inside the cabin. Johnny saw the look in Vascom's eyes, surprised, uncertain for just an instant, and nerved himself to a final desperate effort.

It was not enough. Vascom's reaction was a wild burst of savagery which seemed to give him added strength. And then his weight was even heavier, the knife twisting murderously.

CHAPTER FIVE

Blood spilled across him, and for an instant the world took on a nightmare quality. Johnny threshed violently and threw the oppressive weight off, then sat up, gasping, gazing into a face as white as his own. In its way it was as beautiful as Leavitt Vascom's was handsome, the dark eyes seething with a blend of emotions. They ranged the whole gamut from disgust and rage to revulsion and pity.

Johnny struggled to his feet, looking down at the man who a moment before had been so intent on murdering him. He bent and touched Leavitt, then took a firmer grip on that right arm which had been so menacing, using it as a lever to turn him. The knife had twisted as Vascom collapsed, and now it was buried almost to the hilt in his own chest.

He fell back as Johnny released his grip. Malcolm's mind still boggled at the evidence of his senses. He had seen Vivian Vascom a few times in the past, though not often. She had grown into an aloof, disdainful beauty, reserved, proud, with the arrogance of the Vascoms. Now he regarded her doubtfully, seeing horror in her eyes. She had been away from the country for nearly a year, attending a school in the East. Barney was fiercely determined that his motherless daughter should have the training that befitted a lady.

It came to Johnny that what he had taken for arrogance might be shyness. Her hair was thick and soft and had the sheen and blackness of a crow's wing. Her eyes were stormy as she looked from her dead cousin to him, and she shivered. Her fingers were white from the intensity with which they clasped the butt of a revolver—his own gun, Johnny observed, and understood. She had snatched it up, clubbing Leavitt with the barrel, taking him by surprise. He'd twisted, falling, and the knife had been pointed upward.

Again Vivian shivered, allowing the gun to drop. Her voice was curiously flat.

'He is dead?'

Johnny nodded, sucking air like a swimmer breaking water. His own demise had been so near that his reprieve was still hard to understand.

'He's dead. No fault of yours. It was an accident.'

She looked down again; then she ceased to frown.

'I'm glad,' she announced calmly. 'The insufferable beast! I overheard what you said to him—and what he answered. He was always murderous.'

Johnny could only agree. From his own experience and the many tales he'd heard, the term was accurate.

'You saved me,' Johnny added, and shivered in his turn. 'I'd about given myself up. It was lucky that you happened along.'

'It wasn't entirely by chance.' Her tone was dispassionate, though a fierce undercurrent vibrated through the words. 'That was one time he overreached himself. I got a letter from him, asking me to meet him at the Lampases Spring today. He said that there was something very important that he had to talk over with me, that he had to explain certain things before I talked with anyone else in the family. I've been away, and he sounded quite convincing. So I came. And now I understand what he really had in mind!'

She went on, as though it were necessary to explain, not only for Johnny's benefit, but for her own.

'He was my cousin, of course—but he was always trying to make love to me—oh, for years now. I never took him seriously—I thought it was sort of a game—but apparently he didn't! He wrote me several letters while I was gone. You see—he thought M'Ginnis had money, which he could get through Myra. When it turned out that there was no money, Myra was an encumbrance—to be gotten rid of! By then, Dad had cut him off from any share in Axe, because of all the things he'd done. So he figured still to share in Broken Axe—by getting my share!'

Taken with what Leavitt had said, there could be no doubt that she was right.

'I'm grateful for your help,' Johnny said. 'More than my life was at stake. There's a baby in the house—'

As though on signal, the baby wailed again. Vivian's face had been set and cold. Now it changed, was transformed. She turned abruptly and went inside. Johnny followed.

She stood in the doorway a moment, as he had done, looking about, and he could see reflected in her face the same shock which he had felt. Then she crossed and picked up the baby, blankets and all. The troubled bewilderment was deeper in her eyes as she turned back to him.

'But this—oh, it's awful! I didn't really understand—'

'The baby is probably two or three days old,' Johnny explained. 'Myra said she was starving. I had a can of milk, and I fixed some in that bottle, warmed and diluted. But maybe she's still hungry—'

He turned at a slight sound, then, almost past being surprised, crossed to the bunk. Myra's eyes were open, looking at them. He'd thought that she was gone a while back, but apparently, out of sheer weakness, she had merely been on the verge of unconsciousness. Now she had rallied.

'Now this is better,' he exclaimed. 'You're going to live, Myra, and things will be better. And I reckon the first thing is to give you something to eat, too.'

The soup was warm, and it had simmered to a savory consistency. He found a tin bowl and spoon, and set to work to feed it, a sip at a time, to Myra. Vivian was caring for the baby, working with something of the frantic desperation which had assailed him earlier.

She looked about for some sort of clean cloths which might be used for the baby, and found nothing. Johnny heard its fresh wail of protest as she placed it back in the trunk which served as a crib and went outside.

She was gone only a minute. When she returned, she carried a white garment which he guessed must be one of her own underskirts. Quickly she ripped it into several smaller pieces, then, finding a suitable basin, set to work to bathe the baby. From her manner he surmised that such a task must be as new to her as to him, but she proceeded with determined desperation. Then she clutched the baby, eyeing her handiwork ruefully. But if not artistic, at least it was an improvement.

During all this time, none of them had spoken. Myra had watched, bright-eyed, obediently swallowing the soup, choking once or twice, as though eating were a habit to which she was no longer accustomed.

'There, at least she's clean and fresh,' Vivian observed. Carrying the baby, she crossed to look down at Myra. 'You poor kid!' she added. 'You've had it rough, haven't you? But it's going to be better.'

Myra smiled, but her concern was for her baby. 'Is she all right?' she asked.

'Couldn't be better, considering, though I suspect she's hungry again,' Vivian said. 'But we can do something about that.'

She poured out more of the can of milk and started to warm it. Johnny turned to the door.

'I'll go out,' he said. 'You can tend to things here for a while.'

Vivian nodded understandingly. After some searching, Johnny found what he sought. Even the discovery was a minor shock.

The shovel was a hundred feet from the cabin, behind the clump of screening chokecherry brush. It had been used, not many days before, to dig a grave—the grave which he had expected to toil over. Clearly, on one of his visits there, Leavitt Vascom had been certain that Myra could not last much longer. So he had made grim preparations.

Burial in the hole which he himself had dug was poetic justice, and Johnny wasted no time in ceremony or in consulting the others. Myra was in no condition to take any part, and he was sure that Vivian would not want to. He filled in the hole, then, feeling a strange compunction, picked a handful of wild flowers and placed them on the fresh ground. Strange are the ways of the heart, and whatever Leavitt had been, Myra had loved him. The bouquet was for her.

He found Vivian's horse and brought it up, along with his own. With the thoroughbred, that made three. He was pondering the next problem when Vivian came outside.

'They're both sleeping,' she reported. 'What shall we do next? Myra is dreadfully thin and weak. She should have several days of rest and care before she is moved. And the baby will be hungry—often. I think you fed her just in time to save her. Do you have any more canned milk?'

Johnny shook his head. 'I just brought the one can,' he admitted. 'I didn't count on finding anyone—or anything like this.'

Vivian nodded. 'Neither did I. My horse nickered—and that warned me as well as him,' she added grimly. 'So I didn't ride blindly into sight, for which I'm thankful. You've taken care of him?'

'Yes. He had a grave already dug.'

Understanding for whom it had been intended, Vivian's eyes sparkled.

'Give him one good deed, for which he gets no credit!' she snapped. 'But Myra and the baby must be gotten out from here as soon as possible. That will be the baby's only chance.'

'I'll fix up a team,' Johnny agreed, 'if you think Myra can stand riding in the wagon.'

'She's endured so much already, I'm sure she can.' Vivian nodded. 'It has to be done.'

The team was the real problem. Johnny had been unable to find any harness, but he could contrive a passable set, using lariat ropes. The difficulty would lie in persuading riding ponies to pull a wagon, working as a team. He couldn't afford to have them kick or run away, not with a sick woman and a baby as passengers.

By riding his own horse, as part of the team, he figured to control them. He made a harness, then set about gathering grass and sagebrush as padding for the wagon bed. Meanwhile, Vivian prepared a meal. It seemed a long while since he'd helped himself to the bowl of stew and listened to Howard Denning explain his plan to bring sheep onto the range. His brow wrinkled anew as he remembered Leavitt's slurring reference to sheep.

When other things were ready, he hitched the team, not without difficulty, choosing his own and Vivian's ponies in preference to the thoroughbred. As he swung to his saddle, they took off at a wild run. The wagon wheels creaked dismally, but no grease was available. The spokes, dry and unused while the wagon had sat out in storm and sun, rattled loosely.

Still, it would probably hold together as far as Wagon Wheel. It had to serve.

The ponies were skittish and uncertain, but after a circle of a mile, they lost much of their fright at the squealing vehicle at their heels.

Vivian had ransacked Leavitt's pack and, coupling the contents with supplies from Johnny's, had contrived a good meal. Myra had been completely out of food, even of bare necessities. Ill, in no condition to set out on foot across endless miles, she had been effectively trapped.

They ate; then Johnny carried Myra to the wagon. She was amazingly light, but hope was replacing the despair in her eyes. Vivian carried the baby.

'Where are we heading for?' she asked.

'I think Wagon Wheel's best,' Johnny said. 'It's closest. What do you think?'

'I'm sure of it. Do you have a housekeeper?'

Johnny grinned. 'Not now. Howard hired Lavinia Taylor, after Ma left, and put up with her for a week. Lavinia has a heart of gold—'

'And a tongue that's hung in the middle and works both ways,' Vivian agreed. 'I know. Her talk would drive most people crazy. But there will have to be a woman to look after Myra until she's stronger. She's endured a fearful ordeal, and it will take quite a while.'

'Howard won't object to Lavinia, as long as she has something to do besides talk to him,' Johnny promised. He understood what Vivian meant. In one way, Myra belonged to Axe, but in others she was alien there. For a while, at least, she would be better at Wagon Wheel. Seeing that she was asleep, he spoke.

'You heard what Leavitt said. Myra told me that he came back here and informed her that the marriage ceremony had been a mockery. But she went through it in good faith.'

Vivian's lips thinned, gazing down at the now contented child in her arms.

'Then why should we tell it any other way now?' she asked. 'Let it stand that she is his widow, this baby a Vascom—not that it's much of a heritage! But it's all she has.' She went on thoughtfully:

'Myra won't be able to look after this little tyke for quite a while. So I think I'd better take her until she can.'

'Would you?' He admired her spirit. 'What will your father say?'

'He'll end up by inviting Myra to come to Axe when she is able. He's fair, as he sees things.'

That was probably a correct assessment of Barney, though Johnny could not say as much for Leavitt, or for Slade Vascom, Vivian's brother. Slade and Leavitt, double cousins, made a pair. They had been dubbed the Twins, both because of their physical likeness and their manner of action. The wildness and arrogance of the Vascoms was in both, exaggerated by the lawlessness of the Slade side of the family.

There were no springs in a lumber wagon, and the mattress of grass would not absorb nearly all of the joltings, but that could not be helped. Johnny tied the one horse behind, then swung to the saddle and set out.

The team had run off their skittishness and soon settled to moving ahead in matter-of-fact fashion. It was necessary to hold them to a walk except for occasional good stretches; otherwise the going would be unbearable. But at that pace, it would mean camping that night and traveling on for a while the next day.

In mid-afternoon he knocked over a prairie chicken with a quick shot from his revolver. It would provide a passable supper for Vivian and himself, and the bones, boiled, would make a broth for Myra. The sun shone warmly, and but for the grim background, the trip would have been pleasant. Myra was uncomplaining. Vivian, sitting beside her, holding the baby, would be scarcely more comfortable.

They camped, and he surprised a strange look in Vivian's eyes as she cooked supper.

'So Denning is going into the sheep business?' she asked.

Leavitt's initial greeting had been to call him a sheepherder, and she had mentioned overhearing all that had been said between them. Johnny nodded.

'Howard has decided that this never was cattle country, but should make good range for sheep. He doesn't like the notion, but he's doing it on account of Ma.'

Somewhat to his surprise, Vivian accepted this without comment or further question, with none of the animosity which was ordinarily to be expected, especially from a Vascom.

'How is Ma?' she asked. 'I heard about her accident. I always admired her spirit.'

'Ma has to have another operation,' he explained. 'If it works—she may walk again, may even come back home. If it doesn't—' He let it go at that.

'Then let's hope and pray that it works,' Vivian said. She raised her head, and then he too heard a sound. 'Someone's coming.' After a moment her voice took on an anxious note. 'I think it's Slade,' she added. 'Don't be tricked again!'

CHAPTER SIX

On the Western Wyoming range they had long been called the Vascom Twins, though less complimentary terms were often applied. Leavitt was Old Barney's nephew, Slade his son.

In appearance as in nature, they had been so alike that it had been difficult for strangers to tell them apart. A knife fight had changed that, about a year before. Slade's left cheek had been sliced like steak in a saloon brawl. On healing, the white rim of the scar looked surprisingly like the head of the Axe. It was a mark of which Slade professed to be proud, perhaps to hide his secret distress.

The scar was livid as Slade pulled his horse to a stop and looked about at the preparations for a night camp. Vivian was bent over the cook fire, while Johnny was putting the finishing touches to a makeshift shelter above the wagon box, using a couple of the blankets. Slade Vascom leaned forward, and his breathing matched his horse's. The cayuse showed dark streaks of sweat, and its lungs heaved from running.

'What's this?' Slade rasped. 'What are you doing here, Vivian? We've been wondering why you didn't show up at home—'

He broke off as the baby wailed, as though in protest against the demanding voice. For a moment his face was a picture of astonishment.

'I'm trying as best I can to make amends for Vascom brutality,' Vivian answered. There was no word of greeting, though

Slade's eyes followed her jealously. 'Leavitt deserted Myra when she was sick. She was almost dying when Johnny Malcolm and I found her, to say nothing of the baby.'

Slade swallowed. Clearly this was news to him, and it rocked him. The effect, however, was brief. He fixed quickly on another thing she had said.

'You and Malcolm found her! What are the two of you doing, off here together?'

'I don't know that it's any of your business,' she informed him disdainfully. 'Only we weren't together. We met by chance at the cabin where Myra had been left by Leavitt. Johnny was about his own business. I'd had a letter from Leavitt, asking me to meet him at Lampases Spring. He said it was important.'

The axe-head scar seemed to jerk, almost in a chopping motion. Slade remained in the saddle, his big hands clenched about the horn.

'Blast him!' he breathed. 'And you fell for that?'

'I should have remembered that the Vascom Twins were liars,' Vivian returned bitingly. 'He made it sound important. I rather supposed that you'd been up to more of your usual tricks.'

Slade let that pass, intent on what to him was clearly the main issue.

'And what happened? What did he say?'

'Nothing. I haven't spoken to him for a year. I'm sure he didn't intend for me—or anyone—to find the cabin and Myra. Apparently he had been staying away from it on purpose. Myra was starving, along with all the rest.'

'Starving?' Slade repeated, and for the first time these references seemed to get home to him. He dropped the reins and swung to the ground, crossing to the wagon to look at Myra, still ignoring Johnny. 'I didn't know what the devil Leavitt was up to,' he confessed, 'though he's been acting like a coyote with a hidden den for a long while, and away for weeks at a time. But that was nothing new.'

He stared at the baby, looked more sharply at Myra, and became momentarily agreeable.

'This is bad business,' he admitted. 'He'll have to make amends, or Dad will kill him. And if he doesn't, I'll have a try at it!' he added with a click of teeth, as if the prospect afforded him real pleasure. 'Where is he?'

Myra's voice was tired. 'I don't know. I haven't seen him for weeks.'

'He'd better stay out of sight,' Slade growled, then seemed to lose interest in the subject. 'You're camping here for the night?'

'What else is there to do?' Vivian countered. 'We have to get Myra and the baby where they can be taken care of, but Myra is too weak to go any further today.'

Slade asked more questions, ascertaining that they planned to take Myra to Wagon Wheel, at least temporarily, while Vivian would care for the baby. His face darkened.

'Dad won't like that, and I don't,' he said shortly. 'A sheep outfit is no place for a Vascom!'

Here it was again, the taunt and evidence that the news had spread. Johnny had held silent, keeping a tight rein on his temper, but he could not refrain from an answer.

'Your cousin brought her onto Wagon Wheel range without permission,' he pointed out. 'I'm accepting your word that you didn't know where he was or what he was up to. But there are points where Wagon Wheel draws the line!'

'There's no line so low as that of a sheepman!' Slade retorted instantly. Vivian flushed angrily.

'Slade, you're insufferable!' she protested, and his temper blazed.

'Are you taking his part against me?' he demanded. 'Are you forgetting that you're a Vascom?'

'I'd like to,' she admitted bitterly. 'After all that's happened, I'm ashamed of the family.'

The tension was eased slightly as another rider came galloping up. It was Cy Robbins, who had been an old hand on Wagon Wheel when Johnny had first gone to work for Denning. He looked about in some bewilderment at sight of the wagon and the Vascoms.

'So here you are, Johnny,' he said. 'Howard was beginnin' to get a mite worried when you didn't show up, so I set out to see what might be keepin' you.'

It was decided that Robbins would remain with them until morning, then would ride ahead with word of their coming. Slade was obviously intent on staying also, not at all worried by lack of an invitation. He was barely civil, though he did help gather wood for the fire, and contributed to the supper from his own supplies.

By mutual if unspoken consent, nothing had been said by either Vivian or Johnny concerning what had happened to Leavitt. Myra had been too sick to realize that he had returned. Sooner or later, questions concerning his whereabouts were certain to come up, but it seemed better to add no more fuel to the fires of animosity at this time.

Slade had already saddled when Johnny threw off his blanket the next morning. He rode closer.

'I'm heading back for Axe,' Slade announced. 'One word of advice, Malcolm. You can ride out of this country if you like. I'd suggest you do. That'll keep your nose clean. Wagon Wheel ain't going to be popular in these parts from here on out!'

He put his horse to a fast gallop and was

gone. Johnny rubbed at his stubbled chin, watching him disappear. Coming from such a source, the word might be intended as friendly counsel. Only somehow he couldn't feel it to be so. It was more in the nature of a threat, a warning to get out. Johnny turned to gather wood for a fresh fire.

He left Robbins to drive and rode ahead himself, taking the word to Denning, who listened in understandable amazement.

'I've heard a lot of wild tales about those boys,' Howard confessed. 'And I've seen plenty with my own eyes, but nothing to match this.' He gave Johnny a searching glance. 'I figured there'd be trouble when I decided to run sheep. Now it's a sure thing.'

Johnny answered his unspoken question. 'I'm staying,' he said.

'I knew I could count on you,' Denning commended him. 'You never run away from trouble. I don't need to tell you that I'm glad. But I figure we'll have our hands full.'

Johnny despatched a messenger to bring back Lavinia Taylor. A widow, Lavinia lived with her married sister, and was always available for a job of nursing or whenever a competent woman was required. With her to look after Myra, the business of driving the cattle to the railroad could continue.

'I guess I can duck out enough to keep from bein' jawed to death,' Denning said resignedly. 'One thing about Lavinia, she can be depended on to help where she's needed, even if we're already being called a sheep outfit. And it takes character to do that.'

The wagon made it in about noon, and Lavinia arrived at the same time and took efficient charge. Myra had stood the journey better than Johnny had thought possible, buoyed now by hope.

The baby was again complaining hungrily, and the three women put their heads together over it, assembling an outfit before Vivian went on to her own home, taking the baby. Slade had prepared the way, but it was a strange homecoming when she finally rode up, to be greeted by Barney, his face set and still.

'I'm glad to see you back,' he observed, which was all the welcome she had expected. 'But what's this that I'm told about Leavitt, and him having a wife, and writing to you. Give me the straight of it.'

She responded with an unvarnished account, omitting only the part that Leavitt had been there when she arrived, and what had happened between him, Johnny and herself. Barney listened to her account, looked silently at the baby, then asked a single further question. 'How long before Myra can be brought here?'

'She'll need to rest and get her strength back. Several weeks, I should think, at the least.'

Barney nodded. 'We'll try and have her clear of the Wagon Wheel ahead of the sheep.' His face twisted. 'I never figured to be beholden to that outfit. But life plays some queer tricks.'

He said no more, but one question was answered, and Vivian was relieved. For all her outward air of assurance, she had been far from certain as to how Barney might react to her bringing the baby with her. She sensed that he was not merely accepting what she had done. In his own way, he was proud of her.

CHAPTER SEVEN

The scar on Slade Vascom's face twisted as he rode. It appeared more a grimace than a smile, but to those who knew him it would have passed for a satisfied grin. He'd been jolted by the revelations the evening before, but his suspicions and fears had turned out to be groundless. Some of the developments were even pleasing.

'This time, Leavitt, you really put your foot in it!' He chuckled. 'Which is what comes of grabbing, when you've got both hands full already! Now you've hogtied yourself, and I won't have to worry any more about you. I was beginning to think I'd have to kill you, but it's a safe bet that someone else will take that chore off my hands.'

For a long while, there had been increasing jealousy between them; each had the same prize in mind. Both played a dangerous game for high stakes. Until now, Leavitt had possessed two advantages. One was his unmarred face. Making a virtue of necessity, Slade could boast that as a scion of Broken Axe he wore the brand of Axe, but he was keenly sensitive on the point of his good looks. For appearance, he was convinced, counted heavily in such a game. Women, like men, were often fickle.

The second reason he kept carefully to himself.

He'd been suspicious, frustrated and furious, when Vivian had failed to return home as expected. Though she was far from realizing it, almost everything depended on her. Putting together vague whisperings and rumors, he'd followed a hunch and headed toward Lampases Spring. But he had not been prepared for what he had found.

Since Leavitt had so obligingly eliminated himself from the contest, he could take advantage of the breaks. During the night, lying sleepless, he had evolved a plan. Now he was losing no time putting it into operation.

A small, barren butte thrust ambitiously above the surrounding landscape, three miles north of the buildings on Wagon Wheel. It was still early when a thin wisp of smoke, as from a campfire, rose lazily above the hill.

The smoke hung, drifted, and faded in the brightening glare of the sun. After what seemed a long while, a horseman appeared, riding up a draw, coming without being easily visible to possible watchers. Actually, as Dinty Toole pointed out, he had made good time after discovering the signal.

'I had to get away without anybody noticin',' he pointed out. 'And that takes a bit of doing.'

'No matter,' Slade shrugged, 'now that you're here. I want answers to a few questions. It's sure, then, that Denning is buying sheep?'

'Reckon so. Howard says he's made up his mind. We're to start drivin' the cattle to the railroad any day now. Once they're sold, he'll use the money to buy sheep, and ship them back.'

Slade grew tense.

'Do you know what arrangements he's made to get sheep?'

Dinty gave him a snaggle-toothed grin.

'Happens I do,' he admitted. 'After I got word to you of what he was up to, and you asked me to do some snoopin'—I snooped. Not much trouble about that, with Johnny gone, and the Old Man out ridin'—which he don't often do these days. I pried around in

Denning's desk and found a letter. Sev'ral letters, in fact, but only one that was worth lookin' at.'

'Get on with it,' Vascom said impatiently.

'I'm comin' to it. It was from somebody back in Iowa—I got it all wrote down here, a copy of what I figured you'd want to know. This feller has a lot of sheep for sale. He quoted prices and everything on nine thousan' head. What he was doing was confirming Denning's agreement to buy that many from him, after the cattle are sold. Forty thousand dollars for the sheep, loaded on the cars, ready to ship west. That includes ten experienced herders, who'll go along to look after the sheep.'

'Nine thousand head at forty thousand dollars,' Slade repeated. 'It sounds to me as though he's getting a good buy. Let me see what you wrote down.'

He studied the copy of the letter, frowning, then tucked it in a pocket.

'You've done a good job,' he said and, with unexpected generosity, thrust half a dozen bills into Toole's eager hand. 'This is a bonus, in addition to your regular wage,' he added. 'You say the drive starts in a day or so?'

'That's what the word is. We're just waitin' for Johnny. He rode off on some business and ain't got back.'

'Fine. Be on the watch for another signal.

Maybe you can earn another bonus.'

'I can use it,' Toole admitted. 'One of these days, at this rate, I'll have money enough to buy me a business and settle down. Got my eye on a saloon at Lampases.'

'The Silver Dollar,' Slade guessed. 'The gambling games there pay more than the liquor—the way they're operated.'

'Nothin' wrong with that, is there—so long as a man owns 'em?' Toole grinned. 'I take it that I'm to stay on, workin' for Denning for a spell longer, even as a sheepman?'

'You'd be of no use to me if you left him,' Slade retorted. While Toole returned to his own work, he rode on, keeping out of sight of the buildings of Wagon Wheel, or any rider who might chance along. He paused briefly at Axe to inform his father what had happened, or as much as seemed expedient; then he went on, following a straight line toward the town of Lampases. That the town was roughly half a hundred miles from the spring of the same name seemed to hold no significance or to strike anyone as odd.

There was a bank at Lampases, and Barney Vascom transacted his business through it. Even more vital to Slade's plan was the knowledge that his father had an account of slightly more than forty thousand dollars to his credit.

That discovery, made largely by chance a few weeks before, had intrigued Slade. He had considered a score of plans for getting hold of part or all of the money for his own use, as he had done with lesser sums many times in the past. Certain of those schemes he had worked alone, others in conjunction with Leavitt, who was clever when it came to any planning of doubtful legality. Their success along those lines had led to a memorable blow-up on the part of Barney something more than half a year before. His anger could be terrible, and even the hot-headed Twins had been awed and cowed.

But not for long. There were two imperative reasons, the money in the bank and Broken Axe itself, for further conspiring. Now opportunity was at the door.

It was evening when he reached the town. Slade stabled his horse, found a restaurant and ate, then, under the cloak of settling night, walked to the banker's home.

Slim Bestwick had been a cowboy in his younger days. A riding injury had made it necessary to turn to other less arduous pursuits, and for a score of years, while he lost his nickname and erstwhile leanness, Bestwick had congratulated himself on his mishap. He had discovered an unsuspected talent for business, and for the past dozen years had been president of the bank, as well as its chief owner. He looked up in surprise and with a certain wariness at sight of his caller. But because Slade was a Vascom, he courteously asked him in.

Slade wasted no time.

'I doubt if you'll have heard the news yet,' he said. 'But sheep are due to put in an appearance on our range—at least on Wagon Wheel,' he amended.

Bestwick listened with interest. Though once a cowboy, his years as a banker had conditioned him to think impartially. Once he understood the situation, he nodded.

'I would say that Denning is showing good judgement,' he observed. 'Your range is better suited to sheep than cattle. He'll encounter opposition, no doubt, but in the long run, it should prove an excellent investment.'

'We on Axe think the same,' Slade surprised him by agreeing. 'That's why I'm here. For I don't need to tell you that there's no love lost between Wagon Wheel and Axe.'

Bestwick smiled dryly. 'No,' he agreed. 'You don't need to.'

Since Axe was his client, rather than Wagon Wheel, he could be depended on to respect such confidences.

'Denning has made arrangements to buy forty thousand dollars worth of sheep back in Iowa—nine thousand head. Here is Dad's order on the bank for forty thousand dollars. He wants you, acting as his agent, to send a draft to the owner of the sheep. Denning can buy without knowing the difference. We'll even give him a good break—a quarter of the amount down, the balance in up to ninety days.'

Bestwick considered the implications of the deal for a while, and smiled a slow smile of approval. There were those who in recent years had dubbed him Slick Bestwick, in lieu of the former Slim. He did nothing dishonest, but he approved of cleverness, and this deal had all the earmarks of a profitable transaction.

'I understand, and you may tell your father that I'll handle the matter with discretion,' he responded. 'You may even tell him that I think this is an excellent idea.'

'I think so, too,' Slade agreed, and modestly refrained from explaining just how clever it was, or his own part in it.

CHAPTER EIGHT

The drive got under way at dawn. Having been penned for days in the corrals, the cattle were torn between impulses, anger both to run and to graze the new grass. The cowboys were kept busy controlling them, keeping the herd on the move. It would take ten days for the slow-moving dogies to reach the railroad, where Denning had the promise of cattle cars.

There were good points and bad to such a

transaction as he had in mind. Receipts at the Chicago market were usually scanty at that season of the year, which tended to improve the prices. On the other hand, the herd had come through a long winter, and the leanness of the cold months was still upon them. They would not shrink much on the drive, but neither would there be any reserve of fat to render them attractive to buyers.

Denning was not unduly worried. Chicago was becoming the prime livestock marketing center, and a new practice was springing up in the mid-west, something until recently unheard of. Farmers who had a surplus of corn were discovering that they could buy western cattle, hold them a few weeks or months, feed them bountifully, and round them into fatter, more tender beef than the average customer had ever known. Corn sold in such fashion paid a premium price.

Most of the Wagon Wheel herd would go that way—the calves, cows, yearlings, even some of the older steers. As feeders, they should bring a fair price. Whatever the sacrifice, Denning was hopeful of getting enough to pay needed bills and finance his venture into sheep. Thereafter it would be a greater gamble. If it worked, the big spread which was Wagon Wheel might finally pay off.

Denning had hoped to make the trip back with the cattle, complete his business and visit Ma again. But traveling of any sort was becoming increasingly hard for him, and he had regretfully decided to stay behind, to supervise the work which had to be done in preparation for the sheep, including the building of the corrals and cutting wild hay.

'I'm leaving it all up to you, Johnny,' Denning informed him. 'You'll make the decisions—including what is best for Ma. The doctors have written me, and so has she, but they don't like to say for sure whether or not to risk another operation, and neither does she. I gather it's considerable of a gamble. Well—next to me there's nobody she thinks more of on this green earth than you, and I know you feel the same about her. So I'm shoulderin' that onto you, too. I know you'll do the best you can.'

With a couple of exceptions, all of the crew had agreed to stay on, after Johnny had made known his intention to do so.

Johnny took time to look in on Myra. She was white and thin, but the sickness had run its course. Now, having the hope of life after she had resigned herself to dying, she managed a smile.

'I'm fine, Johnny,' she assured him. 'And I'll never forget what you've done for me.' Her face held a dreaming look. 'I don't know where Leavitt is, but he'll probably try to make trouble. So—take care of yourself, Johnny.'

'I'll do that,' he promised, and said nothing concerning Leavitt. If he was past causing trouble, Slade and others were not. 'I want to see you up and around when I get back,' he added.

'Of course,' she agreed. 'I may be at Axe by then—but if I am, I'll still want to see you, Johnny, whenever you get a chance to say hello.'

'I'll sure keep that in mind,' he agreed, and went out and gave the order to open the gates.

He made lazy progress for a few days, until trouble came from an unexpected source. The trail had grown routine. On this day, following several spurts of sunshine, the sky was obscured, a smell of rain drifting above the dust. The cattle stepped out at a livelier pace, as though suddenly eager to reach whatever destination might be in store for them. They seemed to scent adventure along with the rain, and found both equally welcome.

Watchful riders held them until, at mid-afternoon, there was a sudden belch of a revolver. The blast jarred on the heavy air, and the next instant, bawling, the whole herd surged into motion. It was a stampede, and stampede could be another word for disaster.

Johnny jerked his hat low and settled himself as his cayuse broke into a fast run, understanding this job as well as he. Then he noted incredulously that it was one of his own men who had triggered the catastrophe. Dinty Toole was blowing smoke from his revolver, staring from it to a flopping gopher, then on to the running cattle, which were swiftly leaving him behind.

Returning the gun to his holster, Dinty gazed expansively at the running herd. The clap of sound had worked as well as he'd hoped, producing the same sort of consternation as the rattle of a sidewinder coming from beside a man's foot.

It would be impossible to head the herd or stop them. None of the other drovers were in position to move fast enough. By the time the cattle had run themselves out, they would be widely scattered, and a couple of days lost. These were the sort of aggravations which the Twins paid him to engineer. With luck, he might receive a bonus of up to a hundred dollars for this one, and never would money have been more easily earned.

Strictly speaking, he was not in the employ of Broken Axe; Barney Vascom knew nothing of the deal whereby Leavitt had contracted with him to spy and report anything which might be of interest or possible use against his nominal employer. The idea had been all Leavitt's to begin with.

His own bungling had somewhat altered the situation. Dinty had encountered the other Twin prior to the accident which had resulted in Slade's distinguishing scar;

assuming that he was talking to Leavitt, he had given a report, only to discover that it was Slade. But the error had worked out nicely. For a while, at Slade's suggestion, he had reported to both of them, not telling Leavitt of the new arrangement. Later, they had become joint employers.

He turned in time to catch Johnny's stare on him, and some of the pleasure of the moment drifted away like dust before the wind. He'd get told off properly for such apparent carelessness. But the bonus would make it worth a tongue-lashing.

A new note, in the rising thunder of hoofs and excited bawling of the herd, jerked his head around. Working among cattle as long as he had, Dinty had come to know them well, to recognize the nuances of sound both of individuals and of massed animals. In certain respects they were like people, angry or contented, nervous or placid, and they expressed their moods. Sometimes it was by silence, again by soft lowing, or, as now, by maddened bellowing. Even the tempo of hoofbeats and the clash of horns were full of meaning.

Despite the length of their horns, those did not often clash. A big steer, with a wide sweep of horn, could thread his way at surprising speed through a tangle of trees or brush, scarcely disturbing a branch. Massed, a herd could travel without interfering with one another, save when they chose deliberately to hook or gouge.

Now there was a clash, the shock of bodies. Dinty stared with sagging jaw, bewildered. Here was another change, as swift and unlooked for as the situation his shot had produced.

From where he rode he could not see the cause, but it was clear that the wildly running vanguard of the herd had tried to stop, to turn back upon those who followed, to surge in almost the opposite direction. The gunshot had not really panicked them; it had been more like a signal for a wild dash.

Now their panic was real. Horns rattled as the mass tangled; bawling rose to a thundering crescendo. Then, driven by the sheer weight of fear, they made the swing and came surging back, straight toward Dinty, spreading as they ran, an enveloping, maddened wave of tons of flesh and driving hoofs.

From his own position, Johnny had a better view. The sudden thunder of stampede had surprised the big grizzly placidly going about his own business, with no thought of trouble on so pleasant a spring day. It had been only a few weeks since he had ended his winter hibernation and looked upon the world with a somewhat jaundiced eye. Age carried with it the realization that awakening the new life brought fresh responsibilities, not the least of which was the finding of sufficient food to replenish shrunken flesh and placate gnawing hunger.

Intent on the latter, he had been after a mouse, turning over a rock under which it had sought refuge, capturing it in mid-flight with a darting reach of his paw. The mouse made a tasty but discouragingly tiny morsel.

The grizzly was distracted by the sudden noise of stampede. Rearing high for a better look from near-sighted eyes, he loomed massively in the path of the oncoming herd.

At the same moment, the freakish wind veered. Until then it had carried the grizzly's scent away from the cattle. Now, even as he reared fearsomely, the rankness of bear odor flooded their nostrils.

Sight and smell combined were too much for the cattle. They stampeded back upon themselves; a few of the calves and even a yearling were overwhelmed and trampled in the rush. Then, spurred by terror, not knowing that the equally startled grizzly was hastily scrambling in the opposite direction, they roared toward the petrified Dinty.

His cayuse seemed equally astonished, frozen like its rider by indecision. When the two of them decided that they should be elsewhere in a hurry, the horse started to turn, to swing to the right. Dinty gave a wild jerk on the reins, trying to pull it around to the left.

Jerked savagely in mid-stride, the cayuse swerved, staggered and fell. Dinty went down heavily.

The horse regained its feet in a plunging scramble. Its training had taught it to stop and stand when the reins dropped, but terror of the oncoming herd was greater than discipline. The horse hurtled ahead and was gone.

It had happened in a space of heartbeats. Dinty came scrambling to his feet, tried to run, stumbled and rolled.

Johnny was the only one close enough to see or to do anything. There was a strong suspicion in his mind that the cause of the trouble had not been bungling or thoughtlessness, but treachery. Regardless of that, death was on the move, and such a fate would be a high price, even for a traitor.

He sent his own horse toward the fallen man, forcing it into the path of the herd. The horse knew nothing of statistics, of the countless men and animals who had perished under pounding hoofs in similar circumstances, but its instinct was sure. However, so was its rider, and it obeyed, though unwillingly.

Dinty came a second time to his feet, dazed, his mind numbed by panic. The onrush of the herd was like a high tide sweeping from the sea, threatening to overtop all previous boundaries. He tried to run, but his ankle had twisted in the second fall.

He saw Johnny heading for him, and his guilt was compounded by fear. The foreman had seen and understood his treachery, which had triggered the stampede. And when aroused, the wrath of John Malcolm could be a terrible lash.

Fear supplanted reason. Frantically, Dinty jerked his own gun again, firing at point-blank range.

In that stretch of country there had been no rain for days. The grass was a sparse fringe of green, and dust churned through and around it, stirred by thousands of hoofs. The choking cloud was shoved by the wind, carried ahead of the onrushing herd. In such fog, it was difficult to see.

Johnny watched the raised gun in disbelief; its strike was as swift as a rattler's. Haste caused a partial miss. Johnny had been the intended target, but the bullet buried itself instead in the cayuse. The horse faltered in its stride, staggered and went down, its body a flimsy barrier in the path of the onrushing herd.

Dinty did not shoot a second time. He stared, still with an expression of bewilderment. The barrier erected by his shot might have been imaginary, for the rolling tide did not even falter as it was reached. The cattle were too closely paced, too hard-pressed by their own mates, even to swerve.

Dinty went down a third time, and he did not get up again.

CHAPTER NINE

Instinctively Johnny kicked free of the stirrups, half-jumping, half-rolling clear as his horse went down.

Rolling, he hit the ground, and that part was not too bad, except that the herd was up with him before he could come erect. As though sensing that this might be their last opportunity to run free, they were making the most of it.

A hoof drove like a pile driver beside his face, flicking dirt into his eyes. Johnny grabbed blindly, clutching at a long horn on his other side. His fingers closed near the tip, and the steer reacted violently. A jerk of the head helped Johnny to gain his feet, but also sent him staggering to the side as his hold was lost.

He was bumped from behind and jostled forward, and bumped again, this time from the side. The double motion kept him on his feet, and he grabbed again. This time his fingers found a tail.

For a dozen lurching steps he was jerked along, barely able to hold fast. The press of bodies was steadily thickening, and he could not endure long in so exposed a position.

A fear-frenzied steer ran with half-closed eyes and half-opened mouth. From its throat dribbled a continuous bawling, the sound compounded of anger and terror, along with a sort of resigned acceptance.

Alien scent sucked into the steer's nostrils, only partly smothered by the dust. Reddened eyes made out something alien and therefore to be feared and hated; its head lowered still further, rapier-pointed horns set for a vicious sweep.

The press on either side thwarted its intent. All that the steer could manage was to jerk head and horns upward in violent thrust, not quite where they had been intended. That was a bit of luck. Johnny was caught on nose and bullet-like head between the points, lifted and boosted through the air.

He fell sprawling on the back of the animal whose tail he had been clutching, and again he instinctively wrapped his arms around its neck and clung. Once more the tight press of bodies favored him. His steed bucked as wildly as circumstances allowed, but there was no real chance to show what it could do.

How long or far he could keep riding would be a matter of luck. Skill on a sunfishing bronc was no more than a mild asset here. Even if his mount grew resigned, and he stayed with it, his weight would burden it severely in the long run. Stampeding as these were doing, cattle ran until stopped by exhaustion.

The steer would tire soon. Then it would stumble and go down. If that happened while the press remained heavy on every side, his chances of escaping would be slender. It would be crowding luck past the ragged edge.

His ears caught a mutation in the sweep of sound, a slight ebb at his right hand. Dust was like fog, but the wind sucked some of it away and he could see where the press had thinned and why. Almost beside him was a gulch, its steep side dropping away, the bottom concealed as by fog. The running herd had split almost by instinct, veering to each side to avoid being crowded over the brink.

At least most of them were managing to turn. A scrambling sound, punctuated by a despairing bellow, indicated that at least one had been shoved over the edge. Others might be entering at its mouth and filling the bottom of the draw past the safety point. That was a risk he'd had to take, and Johnny made his choice. He jumped, bunching again to roll, giving himself to the not always tender embrace of lady luck.

His heels struck first, digging into a steep, grassless slope part way down. Branches slapped him, where a bush clung to the slope. A root resisted his plowing spur, holding it an instant before breaking and upending him. He hit the bottom of the gulch on back and shoulders and lay an instant, the breath shocked out of him.

A ghostly cow plunged past, barely missing him, and he clawed and scrambled upright. Farther along the gulch, a scrambling, coupled with the sliding of dirt and small stones, indicated that such animals as had fallen into or entered the gulch were trying to get out.

He put his back to the wall of dirt behind him, able to breath again, taking up as little space as possible. The dust obscured his sight, even as the thunder rolling overhead and on both sides smothered lesser sounds.

Dirt rattled from above, a small cascade pouring over him. There was a possibility of the hoofs which had loosened it coming along, but there was no shelter, nowhere else to go.

The steer came down, sliding, fighting for footing, barely past where he stood. The animal lay a moment, dazed, the whites of its eyes rolling. A horn had caught somewhere, twisted and broken in the descent. Blood poured from the wound, while agony glazed its eyes. Then it got up and went on, weaving drunkenly.

Gradually the thunder gave way to separate, distinct sounds, and then these began to subside. Feeling as shaky as the steer, Johnny followed the draw. He found a calf with a broken neck, then a cow with two broken legs. Surprisingly, he had not lost his gun in all those wild gyrations. He despatched the cow, and ahead was a steep slope, torn ragged by scrambling hoofs.

As he climbed out from the gulch, Cy Robbins rode up. Dust coated him like a blanket, his eyes and mouth making uneasy slits in the mask. He pulled to a stop and stared thoughtfully, fumbling in a pocket for a remnant of tobacco plug, worrying off a corner between teeth which no longer quite matched.

'Thought I heard a shot. Are you real, Johnny, or am I mebby beholdin' the remnant o' your ghost?'

'Now that's a good question,' Johnny conceded soberly. He had no heart for smiling. His near-brush with death and the memory of Dinty Toole were too fresh. The man had been a fool or a traitor, perhaps both. But across the years, Johnny had counted him, if not as a friend, at least as a member of Wagon Wheel and more or less his responsibility. He wouldn't have wished such an end, even for his worst enemy.

'Better climb up behind me,' Robbins suggested. 'Folks 'll think I'm bringin' in a scarecrow.'

The rest of the crew had escaped unharmed. They buried Dinty. Only his gun, which had fallen under him, had escaped unscarred, a crowning irony. As foreman, Johnny spoke a few words above the grave, doing the best he could from memory.

He made no mention, one way or another, of the shots which Dinty had fired. The others, examining the gun, noted the empty shells. They had all heard the first and observed the result, but they, too, kept their thoughts to themselves.

With a fresh horse, Johnny joined the others in the gather. It took a lot of riding, through the remainder of that day and most of the next, to round up the scattered herd. Half a hundred head had died or were so badly injured that they had to be despatched. The stampede had carried them back almost to Termagent Creek, and that meant two days' extra loss.

Those were some of the hazards of the cattle business. A man accepted drought, blizzards, wolves, rustlers and all the rest. Johnny wondered if sheep raising could be any worse.

There was not much doubt but that this was a gesture of warning from some of their neighbors, men who not only resented sheep, but also hated sheepmen. Dinty's final acts had confirmed his suspicion there was a traitor among their own crew. Well, Dinty had collected his reward.

So, too, had Leavitt Vascom, who had been

the first to taunt him with the epithet of sheepherder, who had been a prime mover in the hatred of Axe for Wheel. But such deaths would only spur others to even greater animosity.

Chastened by their tantrum, the cattle behaved circumspectly for the rest of the drive. They even grazed back the pounds lost in running, and appeared in reasonably good condition for the ordeal of the long train ride. There was even a dividend: the cattle cars awaiting them when they arrived. These had pulled in only an hour ahead of the herd; thus the delay due to stampede was no real loss.

Not that time much mattered. A man grew old at a riding job, but so did he if hammering nails or digging ditches, and days and years had a way of blending into the whole, losing significance. There was still plenty of time to sell the cattle, then return with sheep, so that they would be established ahead of the snows of winter.

It was a long chore to load the cattle onto the cars. Again, as during the peak of roundup, the branding and excitement, there was much bawling and concern. Once more the cattle were in a mood to break and run, but now the chance was past. They could fight and resist, and they did. It took nearly two days, and dusk was closing by the time the last car door was slammed in place.

There were two trains. The first one,

loaded, had moved out ahead. Another locomotive, which had shunted a few cars at a time to the proper loading pens, now nudged the cars into a single string and moved to the head. A caboose was at the opposite end.

Four of the ranch crew had gone with the first section. Kid Coffee, Jim Heath and Cy Robbins, along with himself, would go on this one. Johnny did not look forward to the ride with pleasure. Their task was to watch alongside the cars whenever the train stopped, running to cover the length of the train, prodding with poles to force upright any animals which might be down and in danger of being trampled, feeding and watering when they unloaded.

Sometimes a train would start up when a man was halfway along its length. That meant grabbing, climbing to the top and making a precarious way back to the caboose, while the train swayed and jolted.

The remainder of the crew mounted their horses and were lost in the gathering night. In another couple of days they'd be back on the ranch. Far up ahead, the engine hooted.

The train started to move, and Johnny grabbed for the handrail of the caboose. The others, including the trainmen, had already gone inside. There was no one to see him trip on the small wire, invisible in the gloom, which had been stretched taut across the lower edge of the steps. It had not been there a minute before, but it threw him sprawling, writhing, half under the suddenly turning wheels.

CHAPTER TEN

Surprise, coupled with the sudden jerk of the train, almost proved his undoing. As Johnny tripped and rolled, the hand rail at the front of the caboose caught his shoulder and knocked him partly forward, also under. Only his own reaction, twisting desperately shoving back with both hands, saved him. A wheel crunched alongside the high heel of his right boot; then he rolled and was back from under. He came upright in time to snatch the last rail of the caboose, and this time he swung aboard.

For a minute he stood, not opening the door, listening, waiting. But no one came to see, or exhibited any curiosity.

Inside the caboose, the others looked up without surprise, and a comment made it clear that they'd known that he was loitering on the back platform, that he had not missed the train. Kid Coffee was washing his face and hands, making a prodigious splash in a small basin. Cy Robbins was stacking his luggage, and Jim Heath, always a trencherman, had opened a package of lunch and was eating voraciously. None of them noticed his boot heel was scraped.

Checking the next morning, Johnny found the ends of the broken wire still in place. But that again proved nothing. It might be that the man who had affixed the wire was on the train, but too crafty to risk betraying himself by removing it.

The run to Chicago was as tiring as he'd expected, and uneventful. They made a couple of stops to unload, rest and feed the cattle. Even with extra trainmen assisting, it was a long, slow chore each time. They were all dead beat when finally they pulled into Chicago.

There, the news was discouraging. Drought was beginning to lay a heavy hand on some sections of the range, and a lot of ranchers were unloading stock which normally would have been held at least until fall. The market was glutted; it had been having a bad week, and the coming one threatened to be worse. It was a buyer's market, not a seller's.

Like nearly all the other shippers, they had no choice. The had to sell for what they could get.

The decision was up to him. There was no way to reach Howard, and he already had troubles enough. Only a handful of buyers were interested. One, after looking over the bunch, made an offer of forty thousand dollars, which was the minimum that Denning had hoped for. Even then there was a condition. The man would pay ten thousand dollars down, the remainder in thirty days.

The proviso was not hard to understand, conditions being as they were. Time was needed to break up the herd into divisions—beef animals, cows, calves, feeders, and culls—and to find separate purchasers for each bunch.

If he wanted cash, he'd have to take a ten percent discount. They couldn't afford that, so Johnny took the first offer, hoping he could persuade the owner of the sheep to grant them time. He didn't expect much trouble, for ten thousand in cash could be a powerful persuader.

Returning to Iowa, he had a look at the sheep. Even to his inexperienced eyes, they seemed to be in good condition, though he had a moment of doubt as he moved among them. There was a difference, almost as wide as the miles between, between the sparse grass of Wagon Wheel range and the lush meadows where the sheep were now running. Texas-bred cattle didn't always adjust to the rigors of a northern range. The sheep had an innocent, helpless look. Would they be able to make such a transition and thrive?

He was surprised at the readiness with which his terms were accepted. Before the cars were ready, he'd go up to St. Paul, where

Ma had spent so many weary months, and see her. Howard had been back twice, but the intervals between were long.

The antiseptic smell of the hospital, its hushed corridors, were disturbing. It was an alien world, and it must be an added ordeal for Ma. Then he tiptoed into the room, as a nurse cheerfully announced, 'Mrs. Denning, you have a visitor.'

It was plain that Howard hadn't written that Johnny was coming, or if so, he'd beaten the letter. The surprise on her face testified to that. He'd remembered Ma as a husky, hearty woman, a bundle of energy, always flouncing about, equally at home on the back of a horse or in her own kitchen, cheering everyone from Howard to the newest hand who might be nursing a touch of homesickness. The thin form under the sheet, with a touch of gray in her hair and her face to the wall, couldn't be Ma. Then she turned and looked, and as the amazement vanished her eyes lit up.

She didn't rise up, as she would once have done, nor did her voice boom in greeting as in the old days. But it was still hearty, though she choked in the middle of her greeting, and her hand, reaching for his, shook as though its thinness had left it unduly weak.

'Well, forever more, Johnny Malcolm. You old horse thief, you're a sight for sore eyes—and I'll be blessed if mine don't feel like a salt lick!'

She'd toned down her vocabulary as well as her tone of voice to fit her surroundings, but she was the same old Ma, though he sensed how desperately lonely and homesick she was. They talked a streak for a while, interrupting each other. She asked a multitude of questions, which he answered as best he could, until she wanted to know what he was doing there and what was going on at Wagon Wheel.

'I know something is,' she added. 'I had a letter from Howard two or three days ago. What did I do with it? It was here somewhere—I've read it often enough. Trouble is, he didn't say anything. Just sort of hinted at changes, and got my curiosity all riled up. What *is* going on?'

Howard hadn't been able to find the words to tell of his decision, and the news would be a shock. But in the face of so direct a question, Johnny couldn't dodge.

'Brace yourself, Ma,' he advised. 'This has jarred us all—but I think it's the right decision. We've sold off the stock—every last steer, cow and calf. I'm taking back a couple of trainloads of sheep. Nine thousand head.'

She took it better than he had expected. She had always been an understanding woman, and the reason was clear enough to her.

'You're doing all this for me.' She sighed. 'I know Howard. He'd have been willing to struggle along as well as he could, even if he never had a cent to spare. But he's right: it's not good cattle country. Whether sheep will do any better or not—I guess we can only make the try and find out, eh? If the neighbors will let us. Sheep *could* be a real money-maker.'

'I feel that they will be.'

'They'd better.' Ma was herself again, keen-minded, competent. His visit was doing her good. 'I'm that excited at seeing you, Johnny, I'm selfish and forgetful. I've a letter here about you—it came yesterday.' She fumbled under her pillow and this time came up with what she wanted.

'It's from Myra,' she explained. 'Myra M'Ginnis—or Vascom, maybe. I used to mother her a bit, poor motherless lass, and I had a few letters from her, though they stopped a long while ago. Now I'm beginning to understand why. She writes of being stranded on a far corner of Wagon Wheel, of the worthless coot she took up with, and how you showed up in the nick of time to save her baby and herself. There's no word about sheep, or of you making a trip back here. But the things she says about you, Johnny—she makes me proud to know you!'

Johnny was surprised. It had never occurred to him that Myra would write to Ma, as almost her first act once she was strong enough to manage a pen. Apparently the letter had been written so soon after his own departure from Wagon Wheel that there was no fresh news.

'I never had a daughter,' Ma added. 'If I had, Myra would about have filled the bill. Of course she made a sad mistake, taking up with that Leavitt Vascom, but there's no denying that he's handsome as you'd expect a devil to be, and he could be nice enough. I remember the time he tried to butter me up, when first he was making eyes at Myra! But she's had her eyes opened to what a real man is, though it's late—poor lass!'

'She's lucky to be alive,' Johnny said uncomfortably.'

'And well she knows it, and gives full credit to you, Johnny, and remembers you each day in her prayers, which is right and proper. But the Vascoms don't stay squelched, which is what worries, me. Old Barney never turned tail or ran for man or devil. Leavitt and Slade will duck for cover, but they always come back. That's what worries Myra—and me—especially with you taking back a band of sheep!'

'We'll deal with the Vascoms,' Johnny promised. 'You have that operation, then come along home and kick up your heels!'

'If you say it's the thing to do, I'll try it,' Ma agreed. 'Seeing you has perked me up so I can fight again. Bla—bless me, but I feel the same as Myra when she talks about Leavitt.

She says she has about made up her mind to stay on at Wagon Wheel, preferring it to Axe. Leavitt hasn't turned up yet, and she hopes he never does!'

CHAPTER ELEVEN

They were somewhere west of Laramie, and the train was climbing and twisting, crawling through the mountains in the uncertain gloom of midnight, when it happened. Malcolm had fallen asleep, stretched uncomfortably, half on a seat and half in the aisle, with only his boots removed. Even after many days and nights of such journeying, he had not grown accustomed to such quarters.

A jarring crash brought him awake, to find himself on his back in the aisle. The train had stopped with unpleasant abruptness, and loose objects were showering and rattling around and over him. From the outer night came a confused medley of distressing sounds—the terrified blatting of the sheep, along with a grinding noise which gradually subsided. Lesser noises beat like a pulse.

Confused, Johnny fumbled for his boots, and found one of them. He tugged it on, pawing vainly for the other. Not taking time for a further search, he stumbled over obstructions. The interior of the caboose was as black as some of the tunnels through which they had passed. Wrestling open the door, he caught himself just in time, as he was about to jump out.

High white stars in a dark blue blanket of sky revealed the dim outlines of mountain country. They shed just enough light to show that if he got off here, it would be a long way down.

On that side of the track, the slope of the hill fell away, almost sheer. He could not see the bottom.

Other men were fumbling about, cursing at the gloom. A trainman approached, trying to find a lantern which was no longer in its accustomed place. Johnny struck a match, and the glimmer of light revealed not only the lantern but also his missing boot. While the brakie got the lantern lit, Johnny tugged on his boot. On the other side of the car, it was possible to descend to the ground.

Up ahead, confusion attested to the fact that part of the train was wrecked, though for as far as they could see, all the cars seemed still to be on the rails. The air was chill near the top of the divide.

The brakie turned back along the track, breaking into an urgent run as a mournful whistling echoed through the night. The second section of the train was not far behind. A curve shut off the view of their own stalled cars. Unless he could get around it and flag the engineer to a stop, they would come plowing into the rear of their own train.

Since he could do nothing about that, Johnny set off toward the front, picking his way cautiously in the gloom. A few cars were deep in a cut, but most of the train poised on a high grade, with none too much room even to walk at the side.

A whistle indicated that the swinging lantern had been seen; then the beam of a headlight flickered beside Johnny and became stationary. There would be help now from the crew of the second section. And from what he could see, there was need for it.

Sheep were packed in the cars, huddled in a dark mass, some murmuring plaintively. Most of them showed no sign of panic, but waited with a stoic patience.

The track curved again, beyond the radius of the headlight, but he could tell that the hill sloped sharply down at one side. The locomotive of their train, and an unknown number of cars, had been derailed. A dozen cars stood, like drunken derelicts, still upright but with wheels partly off the tracks. Beyond them, several more had plunged and rolled down the mountain. They were scattered in confusion, two or three hundred feet below, and sounds still emanated from them.

This wreck might be due only to a mischance, but there had been too many accidents since the news of Wagon Wheel's plan to change to sheep had become known. What had happened was bad, though it might have been worse. Only a little more would have sent most of the other cars off and toppling.

Had that happened, probably none of the sheep would ever have reached Wagon Wheel; that would have spelled ruin for Howard Denning. It might well be that it had happened already.

Down here, in the deeper gloom, sheep were blatting, some loose and running about in confusion. Several of the cars had broken open, allowing the occupants to escape. Others were still struggling to free themselves. Steam hissed and belched from the locomotive, which lay on its side like a wounded but still dangerous animal.

Johnny found the engineer hobbling about on a strained ankle, nursing a bruised arm with his other hand, but otherwise not appearing to be seriously injured. The fireman had fared even better, which was surprising. They had ridden the engine in its plunge, and both seemed amazed to find themselves survivors.

'What happened?' Johnny asked.

The engineer shook his head.

'Sure and I'd like to know,' he confessed. 'We was rollin' along as sweet as a baby being rocked to sleep, just over the hump, see you, and I was reachin' to ease the throttle a mite as the pull leveled, congratulatin' myself that we'd made the top so easy-like with such a load. And the next thing I knew, we were rollin' and crashin' down the slope, and never a thing to see nor the least bit of warnin'. And Sam was watchin' from his side of the cab, and saw no more than I.'

'Sure, and that's the gospel truth,' Sam confirmed. 'There was a sort of jar, and the old rummy took off and tried to fly, as you might say, and all for no reason that we could tell.'

'What's that?' The voice was sharp, querulous, but authoritative. Several other men had come up, hurrying from the second train. Listening, Johnny discovered that the man who was asking the questions was no less a personage than Van Sickle, the superintendent of the railroad. As chance would have it, he had boarded the second section of the train at its last stop, intending to ride with them as far as Green River.

Van Sickle was in an evil mood. The conductor, with whom Johnny had become friendly, whispered that the superintendent was new at his job; there had been an over-supply of trouble along the mountain division for more than a year, and he had been appointed to make sure that such things as had just happened should not take place. He seemed to regard the wreck as a personal affront.

The running, bleating sheep added to the confusion and his rage. If he was not a cattleman by training, apparently he was by instinct, and he made it clear that he hated sheep. Such business was not good for the country, the railroad, or anyone.

Apparently no one had been seriously hurt, which was something to be thankful for, but Van Sickle was in no mood to be thankful for small favors. They all climbed back, returning to the spot where the engine had jumped the track. It did not take long to find what had caused the disaster.

Upon leaving the rails, the locomotive and cars had torn things up as they went, but enough was left to tell the story. Van Sickle apparently knew his job.

'Somebody loosened a rail and shoved one end of it out of place,' he pointed out, showing where the big spikes had been pried from many of the ties. The spikes had been tossed carelessly about. At night, there was not enough amiss so that a watcher could detect it; and even had the engineer spied the loose rail, there would have been no time, when swinging around a curve, to take action. One set of wheels had found no rail on which to run.

'This was a deliberate trick,' Van Sickle growled. 'They aimed to wreck this blasted sheep train, and they did. Somebody must have known what was coming, and they took this method of seeing that the sheep didn't reach their range.'

Van Sickle issued rapid-fire orders. One man was instructed to climb a pole, tap the telegraph wire, and get a wrecking crew on the move east from Green River.

'We'll clear the track as fast as possible, make repairs, hook on to what cars are still standing, and move them ahead,' Van Sickle explained. 'It's the best we can do for the present.'

'What about the others—and the sheep in 'm?' one man asked.

'Open the doors and let them run,' Van Sickle exploded. 'The sooner we're rid of them, the better.'

Johnny had listened in silence. Now he intervened.

'You can't do that,' he protested. 'That would lose up to a couple of thousand head of sheep, here in these mountains. If they strayed, they could never be recovered.'

Van Sickle swung on him. 'Do you think that would worry me?' he asked sarcastically.

'It should,' Johnny returned. 'The railroad is responsible for delivering the sheep, in good condition, to their destination.'

'Not in the event of wreck, fire or other disaster beyond our cause or control, we're not.'

'Probably you're right about that, though it

might take some arguing in a court of law,' Johnny conceded. 'But if you aggravate the disaster and compound the loss by such methods as you've suggested, the railroad will be responsible, and you'll have to pay.'

Van Sickle turned and thrust closer, to peer at him in the uncertain light.

'What business is this of yours?' he demanded. 'Who the devil are you?'

'I'm Malcolm, foreman for Wagon Wheel, and we own these sheep. I don't object to your releasing the rest of those which are trapped in the cars down below. That will be necessary, of course. But I do want them watched and kept from straying, and our herders will help with that. We'll also have to have help rounding up those which have already strayed. Then they have to be reloaded and sent on, as soon as the track is fixed and the train can run.'

Van Sickle regarded him with bitter animosity.

'You want this and you want that,' he growled. 'You want a wet nurse, don't you? You blasted sheepmen are all alike. No wonder everybody hates you. But if you think that we've nothing better to do than to help chase strays, you can think again.' He stalked away, but Johnny noted that he did not implement the order to allow the sheep to run at will.

From their standpoint, it might have been

worse. This way, they might lose up to a thousand head of sheep, and whether they would be recompensed for them or not was a doubtful question. Such a loss, on top of other expenses, could be a crippling blow. He was sure that it had been planned that none of the sheep should get beyond that point.

Howard Denning had been right when he'd predicted that there would be trouble. But they had expected it to be open, not underhanded.

Van Sickle was coming back, vaguely recognizable in the gloom. He was alone. A shadowy figure suddenly materialized from the darkness between two cars, a club raised to strike. There was not time to make a warning count, though Johnny found himself yelling as he jumped.

CHAPTER TWELVE

The older hands on Broken Axe shook their heads and wondered. For almost the first time in their memory, Slade Vascom was cheerful, even smiling. Still more unusual, he was hard-working, attending strictly to whatever needed to be done. Knowing him, they deduced that something was in the wind.

Knowing himself to be an object of speculation, Slade grinned and was not at all bothered. So far as he was concerned, everything was going well. He had taken a series of steps to insure that it should continue that way. True, John Malcolm had evaded or survived several traps set for him, but luck was bound to turn.

The sheep train would be wrecked in the mountains, and that ought to finish Malcolm and Wagon Wheel at one and the same time. Out of the confusion, arrangements were already made to take over the sheep and dispose of them at a nice profit. It was a change from his original plan, but this was better. There would be a faster return, all going to him.

He knew that his father regarded this change with suspicion, but that was all right, too. It didn't matter overly much how it was managed, just so that he occupied the limelight. The Twins had always been inordinately vain, leading to an increasing rivalry, even for notoriety. Slade took secret pride in a collection of 'Wanted' posters, in which, under **various** aliases, he was the central figure. He doubted if his cousin could match them.

One of these days, everyone on Axe, even Barney—particularly Barney—would find who was really in control.

As he rode by himself, it came as a double shock to encounter a stranger who edged his pony out from the shelter of a clump of brush, a gun held carelessly. Its muzzle, centered on Slade's chest, looked no colder than the eyes behind it. They held the same impartial animosity as a rattler's.

'Suit yourself,' the stranger observed laconically, seeing the temptation in Slade's face, the hesitation as to whether or not he should make a desperation try for his own gun. 'The dodgers read, "Dead or Alive." It's a sight easier to pack in a dead man than a live prisoner. So make your grab—if you feel lucky.'

It had been too good to last, such a streak of luck as he'd been enjoying. Slade decided against sudden suicide.

'If you collect any money on me, you'll do it the hard way,' he promised grimly.

The stranger nodded calmly, kneeing his horse closer. He reached and helped himself to Slade's holstered gun, then frisked him expertly for a hide-out weapon, either blade or shell. Satisfied, he leaned closer a second time, and before Slade could jerk back, handcuffs clicked coldly into place.

'A bold, bad man!' the newcomer jeered. '*And* a desperado, who rambled through the West like a big tornado! That's what they said about you. Why, this will be the easiest thousand dollars I ever collected.'

'I suppose you've a warrant?' Slade asked, controlling his apprehension behind a show of indifference. After all, they were in the middle of Axe range, and there were more ways than one of handling a situation.

'Right here.' The lawman shook his gun before returning it to holster. 'It works.'

'I know you now,' Slade agreed. 'You're Simmons, the bounty hunter.'

'You've got me wrong. I'm Wardlaw.' It was an even more chilling name; it meant that this man had come all the way from California. He had a bulldog reputation.

'Wardlaw fished a folded paper from a pocket, flipping it open with a jerk. It was the mate of one of those in Slade's collection.

'Wanted—among other things—for highway robbery, with murder. You figured you'd be safe here on your home range, didn't you? But when I go after a man, Vascom, I don't stop until I get him.'

'I've heard of you,' Slade acknowledged, and tried a distraction. 'Only this time you've got the wrong man. You really want my cousin, Leavitt Vascom.'

'I'll take your cousin if I can get him,' Wardlaw conceded. 'He's worth just as much. But it was you I came after, and you I've got. That scar isn't to be mistaken. And now we'll turn and head out, avoiding anyone who might be so ill-advised as to try and interfere. Especially ill-advised for you,' he amplified, 'since you're worth as much dead.'

Slade gulped. He'd heard about Wardlaw many times, never suspecting that the bounty hunter would stray so far or dare to invade Slade's home range. The man was as relentless as a weasel, as dangerous as a wolverine. Panic almost mastered him.

'Wait a minute,' Slade pleaded. 'Maybe we can talk this over. I'm worth a thousand dollars if you take me in—but I could be worth more if you don't.'

Wardlaw regarded him inscrutably, and Slade knew that he hadn't been mistaken.

'You figure I can be bought?' Wardlaw asked.

'Any man can, if the price is right,' Slade flung back. 'You've a reputation as a bounty hunter, not as a lawman.'

'Well?'

'So it doesn't make any difference to you, as long as you get your cut. I haven't got the money now, but I will have in a few weeks. Leave me alone, and a little later you can collect two thousand, instead of one—and no trouble about it.'

Wardlow shook his head.

'Hh-uh. I'm not that cheap. Beside, I've come a long way.'

'Three thousand, then,' Slade said desperately. 'You can stick around and take a little vacation. You can't make money any faster.'

The bounty hunter fumbled in a pocket, then twiddled the key to the handcuffs.

'Five thousand, cash, in a month,' he

offered. 'I don't haggle.'

Slade gulped, then nodded.

'Five thousand it is,' he agreed.

Wardlaw edged closer, gun at the ready. He unlocked the handcuffs, returning them to his pocket.

'A month,' he warned. 'And keep in mind that I don't take excuses; only cash. If I don't find the money waiting, I'll take you in—and there are ways of getting the difference out of your hide. Of course, I'm hoping that won't be necessary.'

Nodding, he rode away, forgetting to return Slade's gun to him. Or perhaps it was not an oversight.

Slade was surprised to find himself shaking as he rode home. That had been close—far too near for comfort. That particular murder poster had been plastered all up and down the coast. Because of it, he'd headed back to Axe months before, seeking sanctuary, confident of finding it, as on other occasions. Only things, meaning Barney, hadn't worked as in the past. And now this.

A month wasn't much time to gather such a sum of money, unless he chose highway robbery or a bank stick-up, and he hated to use such methods in his own territory. But thanks to the plan he had already set in motion, it should work out. Still, he had to move fast, instead of with caution, for the stakes were too high to hesitate. His neck was in the balance. The bounty hunter would be back, and it would be impossible to temporize or bargain a second time.

He might denounce the deputy, proclaiming that Wardlaw had agreed to take a bribe. The trouble with such a course was that it would be only his word against the bounty hunter's, and the knowledge of just how badly he was wanted by the law in several other places would come into the open.

A horseman was taking his leave as he approached the buildings; a visitor who obviously had been palavering with Barney. Slade scowled. What the devil had caused Slim Bestwick to ride so far from town?

Drawing a deep breath, Slade entered the house. His hand was being forced, but the show-down might as well come now as later.

In his own room, he kept an extra gun. With his holster refilled, he was outwardly indifferent when Ching Lee, the cook, brought word that Barney wanted to see him.

His father wasted no words. His face was expressionless, but such inscrutability was more threatening than a scowl.

'What's this I hear about you buying sheep?' Barney demanded.

Slade shrugged.

'It seemed too good a chance to pass up,' he explained. 'There wasn't time to consult with you—so I went ahead in your name.'

'So I've been informed. Go on.'

'I got to thinking it over, and decided that maybe Denning was smart. This isn't good cattle country. It ought to be fine for sheep. This was a chance to get hold of the sheep that Denning was aiming to buy. We own them now, though he *thinks* he does. He'll bring them into the country—which others won't like. Wagon Wheel will get the blame. And in the process, it will go broke.'

Barney waited. Slade swallowed and went on.

'We'll end up with the sheep, and they'll cost us next to nothing. By then people will be used to the idea. We can take over the whole range, with no particular opposition. We've fought the Wheel for a long while. This way we'll smash them.'

'Maybe.' Barney made a surprising admission. 'I'm inclined to agree, too, that Denning's right about sheep. This certainly isn't good cattle country. So maybe you're right to that extent. But there's one big difference between you and me, mister.'

Never before had he used the term with Slade. Anger glowed in his eyes.

'I've fought Howard Denning and Wagon Wheel ever since the two of us came to this country, just about together. I wanted the whole range, and so did he. And we always seemed to rub each other the wrong way. But there's one thing about our way—and we've had plenty, one time and another. Denning has always fought fair—and so have I—not in the sneaky, underhanded way that you're proposing!'

'If you're going to cut a man's throat, what's the difference if you do it with a knife or an axe?' Slade demanded. 'Either way, he's just as dead.'

'That I grant. And I don't suppose it makes too much difference to him in the long run. But it can make a lot of difference to the man who does it—whether he's fought fair or dirty. You and your Twin have always preferred to take the dirty way, to stab a man in the back or shoot him from ambush. Oh, don't fool yourself that I don't know what the pair of you have been up to. You've cheated and connived and stolen and even murdered. I suppose it's partly my fault, since I'm your father, and Leavitt has some of the same blood. I tried to bring the two of you up to fight, but to fight fair. I've failed, and I've tried to accept that responsibility, too. But this time you've gone too far—both of you!'

'Preaching comes rather strangely from you,' Slade returned.

'Maybe it does. But I called the pair of you in here nearly a year ago, and warned you that you had to mend your ways or I was through with you. You both promised. You've always been good at promising, but you never keep your word—which is another thing. Until the pair of you came along, a Vascom's word was good. There were no liars in the family. But I suppose that lying goes with all the rest.'

Slade merely grinned. But the cold voice did not change its inflection.

'Months ago, the two of you came sneaking back, after things had gotten too hot for you wherever you had been. I told you then that you could still have a home here if you turned over a new leaf and behaved yourselves. I did it partly from pride of family, partly because I felt that I owed you that much. But I warned you then that as far as Axe was concerned, you were through; that I had cut you out of my will, and neither of you would ever have anything.

'I meant it. My mistake was in giving you another chance. You've both kept on as before, only worse. God help me, I'm ashamed of the name of Vascom, after what Leavitt has done! And now you commit my money, without permission, and plan to double-cross Wagon Wheel as well. This time you've both gone too far. I'm giving you until tomorrow to get off Axe, off this range. And if you ever show yourselves around here again, either of you, I'll turn you over to the law myself.'

Slade did not seem perturbed at the outburst. He was smiling, and suddenly his gun was in his hand.

'At last we understand each other,' he

murmured. 'I don't know where Leavitt is, or care. But from now on I'm taking over here—and there doesn't seem to be room enough for the two of us.'

Barney watched. The shocking thing to Slade was that there was not even surprise in his eyes.

'Put your hands up and turn around,' Slade commanded. 'You'll have to reside somewhere else temporarily. Afterward, we'll see whether you show sense or not.'

He advanced, lashing out suddenly with the barrel of the gun. Barney tried to avoid the blow, but it was too swift. He went to his knees, then onto his face without a sound, while a trickle of blood showed amid the white of his hair.

CHAPTER THIRTEEN

Either he had struck harder than he had intended, or else the old man wasn't as hard-headed as he had always supposed. Barney breathed jerkily, a rasping deep in his throat. Pallor covered his face like a shroud, and his pulse was a feeble flutter. Even when water was flung in his face, he showed no signs of reviving.

Slade worked over him for a few minutes, his uneasiness increasing. Then, when there was no change, he shrugged. Perhaps this was for the better. It could certainly make his plan easier, and it wouldn't be polite to spurn a gift horse. A sardonic grin touched his mouth as he turned, making a quick tour of the house, then going around the buildings.

Except for Ching Lee, busy in his kitchen, no one else was around. The old Chinaman was too near-sighted to see beyond the windows of the cook house, too deaf to notice anything less than a gunshot. Vivian had gone for a ride, taking the baby.

Slade was thankful that she was not around. Being alone simplified what had to be done. He wrapped his father in a blanket, picked him up as though carrying out an old bundle of clothing, and walked to the barn. He deposited the unconscious man on some hay, deep among the shadows of a remote stall. Next he saddled Barney's favorite horse and concealed it among a clump of trees and brush behind the barn. When the crew rode in, they would notice that the horse was gone.

He had barely completed his preparations when Vivian returned, riding slowly. She looked surprised when Slade hurried to meet her, exclaiming as though she had been a stranger.

'I've been wondering where you'd gone to, Vivian. That ride certainly put color in your cheeks—not that they needed it! Did I ever tell you that you're getting to be a remarkably handsome woman?'

Vivian looked at him, startled. This was so unlike his usual attitude that she wondered if he had been drinking.

'Why no, I don't remember that you ever did,' she admitted.

'I shouldn't be that blind—and I'm not,' Slade protested. 'Here, let me help you. I'll take care of your horse. I'll help you down.'

'My, you *are* polite,' she remarked, and handed him the baby, then jumped quickly down. That was not what he'd intended, and Slade scowled, but changed to a twisted grin as she met his look. He even essayed a smile for the baby, who was regarding him with wide-open eyes. The baby promptly gave a wail of displeasure.

'Now what's the trouble?' Slade demanded. 'Most young ladies like me.' Somewhat hastily he handed her back, then protested as Vivian promptly turned toward the house. 'Hey, don't be in such a hurry. I want to talk to you.'

'She's hungry and needs changing,' Vivian returned. 'I'll be in the house.'

Shrugging, Slade cared for her horse, then followed her inside. The baby was occupied with a bottle. Vivian shot a question at him.

'Where's Dad? Have you seen him?'

'Not lately,' Slade said carelessly. 'I believe he rode out somewhere a while ago. Why?'

'Nothing—except that he's been staying

pretty close around the house lately. I don't think that he's very well.'

'You must be imagining things,' Slade protested. 'I haven't noticed anything wrong about him. Anyhow, this gives us a chance to talk to each other. Don't you think it's about time that we did have a talk? You've been away for nearly a year, and I haven't heard anything of your experiences, or how you liked school, or anything else.'

Vivian looked surprised. 'There's nothing to tell,' she said. 'School was all right, I suppose, though I felt rather out of place back there. But I didn't suppose that you had the slightest interest in what I did.'

Slade looked pained. 'Whatever gave you that idea?' he asked. 'Of course I'm interested in what you do, or have been doing. I care more about you, and what happens to you, Vivian, than anyone else. I always have.'

That was news to her, and again she wondered if he had been drinking. Slade went on eagerly.

'I guess I understand, and I suppose you got the notion that I didn't care too much about what went on around here, because I didn't take much part in helping with the ranch. But that's not because I didn't want to. You know how Dad is—he always likes to run everything to suit himself. At least that's the way it was. I think things are changing some now. We've had some talks, and I'm to do more from now on, take a bigger part in running things.'

Vivian regarded him uneasily. He sounded nervous and disconnected, but he had been unpredictable most of his years.

'Dad can use more help, I'm sure,' she murmured. 'Axe is a big place.'

'There's no question about him needing help. From now on, I'm really going to take an interest—and that includes you, of course. For this affects both of us, Viv.'

She could smell no liquor on his breath, but he was increasingly strange. Vivian moved to put a table between them.

'Does it? Well, of course we're both interested in things, I suppose—'

'Of course we are, but it's a lot more than that.' He moved quickly to one side, and as she countered by turning the other way, darted back and was beside her. 'Don't you understand? I'm interested in *you*!'

She was suddenly frightened, but strove not to show it. She managed to laugh.

'That's certainly a change, that you should know I'm alive, Slade. But I don't understand—'

'You might as well then, and now is as good a time as any. For I can't go on the way I've been doing any longer. You mean too much to me. You're not really my sister, you know.'

This time she was really surprised.

'You're my half-brother, if that's what you mean,' she returned. 'I've always known that, of course—'

'But that's just it. We're not,' he said triumphantly. 'I mean, I'm not your half-brother. Actually, we're no relation at all. I suppose that technically we'd count as stepbrother and sister, since Dad married your mother. But you're really no relation at all. You were a baby at the time. I remember you—and how you wanted your own way even then!'

She stared at him, beginning to comprehend, and all at once a number of matters which had puzzled her became understandable.

'I didn't know that,' she admitted. 'I didn't realize. I just took it for granted—'

'Sure you did, as was natural,' Slade agreed, and grinned at her triumphantly. 'But that's the way it is. Now do you see what a difference it makes?'

She understood clearly enough, and her dismay increased. But it wouldn't do to let him see that she was afraid. She shook her head.

'I can't see that it makes much—after all this time.' She was careful to hide the sudden feeling of elation which countered other emotions. It made no particular difference that Barney was not her father. She had always respected him, but had sometimes felt guilty that she could feel no real affection for any of her relatives. That was more understandable now.

As to Slade and Leavitt, her feeling for them had been one of active dislike, increasing rather than diminishing as time went on. Leavitt now lay in a nameless grave, and indirectly it was because of her. But she could feel no sympathy or contrition, when she remembered how he had held a knife at Johnny Malcolm's throat, the way in which he had treated Myra, and the rest.

'It makes a lot of difference.' Slade broke in on her thoughts. 'I never said anything about how I felt before you went away—I guess I was too scared of the Old Man to dare speak up. And since you've come home, I haven't had a chance. But now you understand how things are, and I can admit that I've always loved you, Viv—and not as a brother! Now we can get married, for there's nothing to prevent it.'

He grabbed for her, and she dodged behind the clothes basket in which the baby lay. She could not hide the horror and revulsion in her face.

Slade tried to dodge again in the opposite direction to intercept her, but this time the baby set up a wail. Frustrated, he stopped and she bent to soothe the baby.

'Now see what you've done!' she protested, and managed to keep her voice even, almost light. 'You'll have to give me time to think about this, to get used to the notion. It's all so new! We're still brother and sister—at least—'

Slade scowled at the baby. 'We're not,' he growled. 'We never have been and never will be. I thought you could tell how I felt about you, even if I didn't come right out and say so. Why, Viv, I've been crazy about you for almost as long as I can remember—'

'You're talking crazy now,' she protested. 'I couldn't even think of such a thing—'

'Why couldn't you?' Slade's voice was thick with sudden jealousy. 'What was there between you and Malcolm, when I found you together off there? Don't tell me you've fallen for a dirty sheepherder like him—'

'That will be enough, Slade!' She had been raised as the daughter of Barney, and no one had ever suggested that she lacked the Vascom pride. On occasions, as now, her anger could match theirs, too. She blazed at him, and Slade retreated, discomfited. But his suspicion was fanned to a virtual certainty.

He retreated to another part of the house, then went on to meet some of the returning crew members. Some of them were loyal to Barney, and would react suspiciously to anything which he might suggest. But there were others, in addition to certain employees at Wagon Wheel, who had taken his pay for a long while. The time was at hand for such men to earn that money.

CHAPTER FOURTEEN

Johnny's yell mingled with a triumphant exclamation from the club wielder as he jumped and swung at virtually the same moment. He could not forbear to vent his spleen in words as well as action.

'So far, Malcolm, you've had the devil's luck, but try and get out of—'

There was no path, there at the rim of the railroad grade where Van Sickle walked. Below that, the hill fell away steeply. A likely spot for murder.

Johnny's shout warned the killer that he'd misjudged his man in the dark, but frustration only spurred him on. Malcolm's shoulder hit the railroader, twisting him partly about and shoving him back, but there was no time to avoid the blow originally intended for himself. Johnny took it on his upflung arm, grabbing.

His fingers met the club, and it came free in his grasp, while he reeled at its shock along his shoulder. He staggered; his legs twisted and his feet fumbled. Then a hand caught him and pulled him back as he reeled, and he realized that it was Van Sickle, aiding him.

Their antagonist was gone, ducking

between two of the cattle cars and through to the far side of the track, immediately lost to sight. Van Sickle pursued, but presently came back. By then, the numbness in his arm was receding, and with only a torn shirt and swelling bruise, Johnny decided that it could have been worse.

'You all right?' Van Sickle asked gruffly. 'He got away,' he added.

'I could be worse off,' Johnny returned. 'That was what he aimed at.'

'He mistook me for you, and would have smashed me off there if you hadn't jumped in,' the superintendent fumed. 'What the devil's going on, anyhow? First this wreck—then this. They must have a connection.'

'Seems likely,' Johnny conceded dryly.

'I lost my temper and made some uncalled-for remarks,' Van Sickle confessed ruefully. 'But it strikes me that this is going pretty far, even for a row between rival outfits.'

'I'll go along with you on that,' Johnny agreed. 'A lot of it seems pretty personal, which has got me to wondering. I'm only foreman for Wagon Wheel, but it seems almost as if the sheep were only being used as an excuse.'

'That's an interesting notion. You have some special enemies, or something?'

'I didn't know of any. That's what keeps

me guessing.' He was searching his memory, trying to place the voice, but without success. It had sounded familiar, but the impression was as elusive as it was hazy.

'My guess would be that whoever tampered with the rail was still hanging about, and when that failed to get you, he saw this chance and took it,' Van Sickle observed. 'As it is, I owe you an apology, as well as a solid skull. Maybe it's too thick to have been damaged,' he added with a grin. 'But I'm partial to keeping it that way. We'll look after the sheep as well as we can. You give the orders where they are concerned.'

The herders were arriving by then, and by morning, under Van Sickle's steady drive, most of the strays had been rounded up and the track cleared. By mid-morning they were ready to roll again.

He was somewhat surprised to find neither Howard or any others of the crew awaiting them when they unloaded the sheep for the drive to the ranch. There would be a lot of work on Wagon Wheel, building corrals, putting up hay for winter, doing a score of unaccustomed chores in anticipation of the new role for the ranch. Still, he'd expected some word.

The sheep, divided into two big bands, moving a day apart, were not so hard to handle as he'd feared. The herders and their dogs were skilled.

They had covered half the distance to Wagon Wheel before real trouble loomed on the horizon. A dozen mounted men rode into sight, well armed. An eager look dashed Johnny's hope that some might be from Wagon Wheel. And while none belonged to Axe, it required no imagination to guess that Axe would have influenced the men to undertake the mission. Some of them had been friends, but that, he suspected, was definitely in the past.

Johnny rode to meet them, Cy Robbins beside him. Big Bill Leseur led the deputation. He held up a hand in a flat gesture as Johnny approached, the signal as negative as his voice.

'You've come far enough with those sheep, Malcolm,' Leseur warned. 'You ought to know that we won't allow anything of the sort in this country.'

'I've been expectin' some such word,' Johnny returned with equal frankness. 'But aren't you overlookin' a couple of factors, Bill? All the land hereabouts is open range—and we have as good a right here as you or anyone else. And I mind me of an old saying in this country: that it's a free country for everybody.'

Leseur shook his head.

'That don't apply to sheep or sheepmen.'

Johnny looked surprised. 'You mean you're settin' yourselves up as judge, jury and law—above the government?'

'I mean we ain't going to allow sheep to reach our range.'

'They won't be on your range any of the time. I'll promise you that. Once on Wagon Wheel, we'll make sure they don't trespass or bother anyone else.'

Big Bill's headshake was uncompromising. 'No!'

'I could suggest, Bill, that you might be first cousin to a Missouri mule—but one or the other of you might take that as being uncomplimentary, so I won't.' Johnny grinned and looked around.

The herders had left the sheep to be held by the dogs, and were coming up. Johnny had said nothing to them, but they had a good idea of the situation. For the first time, he noticed, they had buckled on guns. With them, the two forces were approximately equal. And it didn't really make any particular difference whether you thought of things as a cattleman or from the point of view of a sheepman. Your reactions were the same.

'I don't intend to start trouble, Bill,' Johnny went on, and was conscious of a surprising feeling of kinship with the herders. 'But you know that Wagon Wheel has never been pushed around.'

The others hesitated. As he expected, this show was by way of warning. It seemed to come home to them that they were being used as cat's-paws, and they had no relish for what might prove a bloody clash.

'Our job was to warn you that you've come far enough,' Leseur said. 'We've done that. You keep on at your own risk.' He led his men away, retreating with reasonably good grace.

As evening came on, there was still no sign of Denning or any of the main crew. But other men came out of the night in force, shadowy figures on horseback materializing suddenly, outnumbering them three to one. Most of them Johnny recognized, and knew that the preliminaries were over. These were riders of Axe.

The first intimation of their presence was a voice, calling warningly from the gloom.

'Don't make any wrong moves and nobody will be hurt—aside from your boss. Every man of you there is covered by a gun. Start trouble, and you and your sheep are finished. This is by way of warning, since you wouldn't heed a friendly word. We don't want bloodshed.'

A hush followed. In it, everyone could hear the clicks as hammers were thumbed back on six-guns or from rifles. The sounds echoed from every side. The voice spoke again.

'A couple of your men can walk around and check, if you like, just to see that we ain't bluffing.'

Johnny knew that it was no bluff. Broken Axe, like Wagon Wheel, never bluffed.

'You see how it is,' the speaker added. 'Start anything, and you haven't a chance. But we aren't hurting anyone—not even the sheep—right now. Nobody but you, Malcolm. You're boss here—as well as being a traitor and a dirty turncoat. So we'll make clear what we mean.'

A quartette of shadowy figures advanced out of the gloom, each with a leveled gun. It would have been suicidal to resist. As one man helped himself to his gun, Johnny's nostrils caught a new odor—sticky and almost pleasant, save for its connotations. It was the smell of hot tar.

CHAPTER FIFTEEN

The ranch house on Wagon Wheel was a sprawling but comfortable two-story affair. The weather had turned hot and dry, and Myra's room, on the second floor, was breathless. Through the open screened window, a cool night breeze tempered the room's atmosphere. Lying wakeful, Myra thought of many things.

There was her baby. Vivian had sent word that the child was doing well, and she would bring it back some day very soon. Myra's strength would permit her to care for it again. She was able to be up for several hours each day, even to take walks out of doors. It was almost like a miracle to be alive.

Slade Vascom had come to Wagon Wheel and asserted that he was taking Myra home with him, to Axe; he'd demanded to talk to her. Myra had overheard the altercation, the raised voices as Howard Denning refused and warned him to get off Wagon Wheel and stay off. Slade had sounded so much like Leavitt that she had shivered in fear. But he'd gone away again.

She had come to like Howard even to respect him. Now she admired him, for he had stood up to Slade, although he was a sick man, scarcely able to stir from the house. He was waiting for Johnny Malcolm to return, to look after affairs. She hoped Johnny would not be long in coming.

Myra started, hearing his name, Johnny Malcolm. Someone had spoken it in the darkness outside the house. Two men were talking, speaking in hushed voices, but sound carried in the silence of the night. Since her window was up under the eaves, they could not see it, or suspect that it was open, that anyone might be able to overhear.

'Yeah, he's on the way with the sheep. But they've come about as far as they'll get. Axe is set to see to that. They're going really to take care of the sheep—and Johnny—tomorrow night.'

The voices drifted into silence, but terror was in the dark room now. Axe wanted to get Johnny. Axe had become a symbol of fear, something beyond scruple. They would kill him.

She must do something, but what? Those men had belonged to the crew of Wagon Wheel, but their words had made it plain that they were in the pay of Axe, turncoats, traitors. Who could be trusted? She dared not tell Howard, for he'd try to ride himself, even if it killed him.

She was up, fumbling for her clothes, dressing hastily in the darkness, not daring to strike a light. There might still be time to ride, to reach Johnny, to warn him, to help. She was not too strong, but well enough, and this was a task which had to be done. Silently she let herself out into the night.

Night had fallen when Slade Vascom rode out from Axe, leading a second horse on which Barney slumped like a half-emptied sack of grain. He had not regained consciousness, which under the circumstances was convenient. Though he had struck harder than he intended, Slade had no compunctions. Not only did this make the present operation easier, but this was a long overdue payment for wrongs, real and fancied.

His hatred for his father, coupled with

sometimes passive, often open rebellion, dated back to a spring blizzard when he had been eight years old. He remembered vividly, partly because it had been his birthday. His mother had baked a cake. For a present, and because she had been raised a Slade, she had given him a six-shooter—a woman's model, small and dainty, but deadly. It was the first gun he'd ever had. Slade remembered his wildly exultant thrill when he had held it in his hands.

For his Twin, Leavitt, who thought his cousin was so like him, there had been a gift also, by way of compensation. Leavitt's mother and his own had been twin sisters, Slades. In their eyes, that was like a badge—not a blue ribbon, but a red.

Leavitt's gift had been a small, perfectly honed model of a standard bowie knife. Already, Leavitt had shown his fondness for such a weapon, practicing endlessly with an old jackknife, literally chopping a board to splinters. That same evening, in the gathering dusk, he had transfixed a rabbit with his new blade, blooding it properly.

Along with the cake and the gifts, Slade's mother had told them the story of her father—their grandfather Slade and his exploits, as a young man. Like most of the Slades, he had died young, at the end of a rope. But she had made him appear a heroic figure, one to be emulated. Both boys had listened, enthralled.

Barney, who had been young them, had been out on the range all day. He had returned, soaked and chilled and in a bad mood, in time to hear Leavitt's squeal of glee as his knife transfixed the rabbit, to find the boys dancing about the victim, shaking knife and gun in a sort of ritual. The sight of the weapons in their hands had enraged him.

He'd stormed into the house, accusing his wife of wanting her children to follow in the steps of their grandfather. His tone of voice, more than the *words*, had conveyed his contempt and disapprobation for the man the Vigilantes had hanged.

Slade's mother had screamed back at him. Then, while he went to change to dry clothes, she had moved swiftly, slipping out of the house with both children, fumbling in the gloom of the barn, saddling two horses, one for them, one for herself. Slade still remembered the creaking and groaning of the boards in the wind, the thickening storm. He had been frightened, but like Leavitt, he had obeyed without protest when she loaded them onto one horse and mounted the other herself, heading out into the darkness.

It had been raining as they set out, but soon the rain had changed to sleet, then to driving snow. A late spring storm could sometimes be worse than midwinter blizzards, and this was such a storm. Before an hour had passed, all three had been shivering, chilled to the bone and lost. He suspected that they would have turned back, had any of them been sure which way to go or what to do.

It had been past midnight before his father had found them. By then, one horse was down with a broken leg, the other shaking with exhaustion. The injured horse had caught its rider when falling. It had come to both boys, shockingly, and only minutes earlier, that she was dead.

From that day, they had hated Barney with a bitterness which never wavered, holding him responsible, clinging to the teachings of Slade's mother as the only true faith. Their goal had been the emulation of their grandfather, and whatever Barney Vascom had done, all that he had tried to teach them, had been scorned.

Had his second wife lived longer, she might have made a difference, even in them. She had been a proud woman, fitting well into the tradition of the Vascoms, but gentle, with a sweetness which, against their will, had won the boys. But that was two years later. Her small daughter, who had become Slade's stepsister, had been a toddler, just learning to walk.

Their stepmother had been with them only a couple of years, not long enough to overcome former memories or deep-hidden resolutions. Pneumonia was as swift a killer as it was deadly.

Slade found himself remembering as he rode, and feeling an odd sort of regret. Like an imperfect kitten, it had taken him a long time to get his eyes open. By then it had been too late.

He no longer thought of his grandfather as a heroic figure, or one to be emulated. Plenty of men remembered and still spoke of him and his exploits, seldom realizing that he had been any kin of the Vascoms. Drew Slade had been a gunman and killer, too cowardly to give opponents an even break. Slade recognized his own heritage, the taint in his and Leavitt's blood.

As for his mother—well, the less said of her the better. She had been beautiful, wild and tempestuous, and such qualities had appealed to the hot-headed Vascom boys, Barney and Phil. Phil's wife had left him and her son, to run off with a wagon train boss headed for California. Phil had caught up, only to find that he was up against a faster gun than his own.

Barney had wanted them to amount to something, which had probably been his reason for risking marriage a second time, to give them the influence of a good woman. During most of the time she had been with them, they had resented their stepmother, remembering a stark figure in a driving blizzard.

Slade shrugged, glancing toward the slumped figure in the saddle. It was too late for such thoughts, much too late, with the bounty hunter set to return. He could see now the rightness in Barney's philosophy, how much better it was to be the honest, respected owner of a spread than to be a man on the run, always looking over your shoulder. There was no glamour in such an existence; only misery.

But he, like Leavitt, had journeyed past the point of no return. Barney had finally drawn a line, after repeated warnings, and they had overstepped it with cool deliberation. Regrets were as useless as tumbleweeds. He was his mother's son, his grandfather's scion, not Barney's, and it was his neck, like his grandfather's, that was in danger.

The simple way, and perhaps the best, would be to strike again, then dump the body into some draw where only the wolves would ever find it, and be done. Two things stayed his hand. He had already set plans in motion, and Axe's crew was riding. Life was unpredictable, and events. Barney might possibly prove useful.

The other, less tangible, was the memory of how Barney had taken off his own heavy coat and wrapped him in it on that long-ago night of blizzard, after wrapping Leavitt in his aunt's coat. Somehow he had contrived to carry both of them in his arms, on the horse, back to shelter in the grayness of dawn.

I might even give him a chance, if he comes around and agrees to be reasonable, Slade reflected. Just so I control Axe and Wheel.

Twice chilled to the bone in a matter of hours, staggering with exhaustion, his father had been unable to ride back to where the dead horse and woman lay in the blizzard's path; or even to give coherent orders to his crew to go after his wife. He had come down with pneumonia, and lived. But by the time he had become rational again, the weather had turned warm, the snow had gone, and the wolves had ranged widely. That too, the boys had held against him. Yet now, for the first time, Slade grudgingly admitted that he had done all that was possible.

It was past midnight when they reached the cabin beyond Lampases Spring. Slade had never visited the place, but he knew about where to look. Leavitt had taken Myra there, had held her hidden and a virtual prisoner for half a year, and no one had been the wiser. It would be ideally suited to his own purpose.

He untied the still unconscious man and half-carried, half-dragged him inside the cabin. With the door open, a thin glimmer of moonlight came through, enough to reveal the bunks along one wall. He got his father into the lower one, and his thoughts turned sardonic. This was where Myra had preceded them.

The sun had taken the place of the moon when he awoke, at a sound from the lower bunk. Barney was not only conscious but awake, which attested to the hardness of his head and the toughness of his constitution. He'd come through a lot which would have killed lesser men; under the circumstances perhaps that was a pity.

Reaction had left him weak and a little dazed. He looked about uncertainly as Slade swung down from the upper bunk. His glance ranged the cabin, and understanding came into his eyes.

'So this is where you've brought me.'

Slade nodded, and erased all weakness or sentiment from his tone.

'I'm giving you one more chance. If you give *me* another, you can go on living. It's as simple as that.'

Barney contrived to shrug. The gesture brought a grimace as pain raced through his skull, and he sank back. But his whisper was defiant.

'There's an end to the longest rope.'

'Think it over,' Slade advised. 'I can get along without you—but you can't without me. Not this time.' He took a considering look around the cabin, making sure that it was as barren as the others had reported.

Outside, he studied the door, walked around the cabin, and was satisfied. It was old and ramshackle, but still sufficiently sound for his plan. There was no window. Once the door was barred on the outside, it would be an effective prison. Lacking any tools with which to dig, cut or batter, even Barney, tough as he'd proved himself, could not escape.

Slade barred the door, then looked for the spring. It was not difficult to locate, but what he saw not far beyond startled him. He needed only a glance to be sure that it was a new-made grave.

Its significance was clear. There was even a dried bunch of flowers on the dirt, had additional proof been needed. Here, almost certainly, was the answer to the continued absence of Leavitt.

And it makes sense, Slade reflected. Malcolm found him here—or the other way around. In either case, Malcolm killed him, which is surprising, considering Leavitt's way of fighting. But I guess I owe you a vote of thanks, Malcolm—not that I'm going to give it. This simplifies matters in more ways than one, and I certainly won't shed any tears.

He returned to the cabin and cooked breakfast from his supplies, giving some to his father. Barney had no appetite. Recovery would be slow, even under good conditions.

There was an old shovel in the brush, which had already been used to move the dirt. Disliking his task, but knowing that it might be useful, Slade set to work. At least it was easy digging, and once he had come upon the body, the wound was clear enough so he was certain of the cause of death.

It would be convenient to have witnesses, but that was out of the question on several counts. He filled the grave in again, then returned to the cabin. Barney had apparently been asleep. He looked wan and feverish. Slade sat on a stool and reported.

'I found Leavitt,' he explained. 'Buried, off up the gulch. He must have tangled with Malcolm, and his luck ran out.'

'Good for Malcolm,' Barney observed. 'It saves the hangman a chore.'

Slade did not contest the sentiment. After what Leavitt had done, he was inclined to agree.

'That solves part of my problem. I'll have to be getting back to Axe, taking charge. You know, I've been thinking. I guess I've been mistaken about you in some ways. That's neither here nor there, except that you can still have a place there if you want. Only I have to run things.'

'The answer is still no.'

'Suit yourself.' Slade stood up. 'Maybe you'll change your mind, after thinking it over a few days. There's water in the bucket, some grub in that sack.'

He bolted the door again, and squinted at the sun. In another few minutes that side of the cabin would be in the shade, remaining so for the rest of that day. But on the morrow, the sun would shine hotly again.

From a pocket he took a small magnifying glass with which he and Leavitt had played as boys, starting more than one fire over which to roast game or fish, feeling like pioneers because they had no need for matches. He cut a crotched stick and thrust it into the ground, then fastened the glass in the crotch. It was a simple matter to focus the beam of the sun onto one of the tinder-dry logs near the corner of the cabin. After a minute, a thin streamer of smoke started to curl, then died as the shadow shut away the sun until another day.

He gathered an armful of dry wood from among the brush of the gulch, piling it in place, and several handfuls of cured grass from the previous summer. These were about the stick, stacked against the logs. There would be no stick left as evidence after the sun focused again, and if the magnifying glass should ever be found amid the ashes, it would be so twisted and melted as to be unrecognizable.

It was unlikely that anyone would see flame or smoke on that remote corner of Wagon Wheel range and investigate. Should anyone do so, he would be back on Axe, busy about other matters, when the fire was discovered.

CHAPTER SIXTEEN

Johnny stood rigid. The quartette from Axe had guns on him, and there were others all about, keeping a sharp watch on his own men to stop them from interfering. It came again, more forcefully now, that there was an element of the personal in this, directed against himself; something more than dislike for sheep or for the foreman of Wagon Wheel.

Now it was driving toward culmination. One of the four men carried a bucket, and it was from this that the sweetish smell of warm tar emanated. A second man had a bulky sack slung over his shoulder, and Johnny could guess its contents.

It was folly to fight back when the other fellow had the drop, when you knew that he had no scruples, and would welcome an excuse for pulling the trigger. To submit was common sense. But there was a point where good sense left off, and this was that point.

He went into action, jumping straight-armed, the drive of anger behind the blow. It caught one of the men and sent him sprawling, his nose gushing blood, his gun lost in the gloom.

Johnny spun, using a trick which had been tried against him and which was deadly if properly worked—kicking and twisting, raking with the spur. It could be as vicious as a bowie.

He aimed for the man with the tar, but another came out of the gloom and got in his way, then cried out sharply as the spur slashed with a ripping of cloth. He grabbed frantically at the tormenting leg, caught Johnny's foot and held, twisting. Johnny sprawled, and others piled on him like ants swarming over a bug.

Johnny outdid the insect struggling. Twice he almost broke away, and once he closed his fingers on a holstered gun and got it loose, but before he could bring it into action another gun barrel slashed alongside his skull. He fell back, his head feeling as if it had just been cleaved, pain bursting through the top of his skull.

As from a long way off, Johnny heard the voice of Cy Robbins, methodically cursing his captors. No one paid much attention. Wagon Wheel, the sheep and the herders were incidental. It was Johnny they were after, and they had him.

They ascertained that he was not too badly hurt, and that pleased them; they wanted him to feel, to suffer his degradation to the utmost. They dumped the bucket of tar over him, turning him so that he would be more completely covered. One man took hold of his boots, another caught his arm, and they lifted, twisting, turning, sloshing him in what had spilled.

It soaked into his clothing, clung and held. The sack was upended, spilled in a fluttering cloud. A torrent of feathers stuck and clung until he was like some grotesque fowl.

His head cleared slowly. Blood trickled from a cut in his scalp down the side of his cheek, along his chin. Some reached his mouth, rank and salty, flavored by tar.

The sheep stood uncertainly, an endless cacophony of sound drifting like a wail from thousands of throats. The bleating held apprehension and fear of the unknown.

Someone got hold of and lifted Johnny, growling at the tar, and let him drop back. That gave them an idea, and they discussed it with the hunger of dogs for a fresh bone. He would not be subjected to the final indignity of being ridden on a rail. For one thing, there was no rail handy. And there was something better, or worse, according to the point of view.

A couple of men picked him up, trying to hold where there was not too much tar. They partly dragged and partly carried him, and again he heard the voice of Robbins, cursing, protesting, until it was suddenly cut off.

The sheep shied, but stupidly, not far. They were pressed too closely to move much. There was nearly five thousand head in the band, and the men were dragging him to the center of the mass. There they dropped him, then made their way back out. Wild yelling signaled the final act, to scare the sheep. They were to be stampeded into frenzied movements, with him helpless in their midst.

It seemed to Myra that she had been endlessly on the trail, finding no one, getting nowhere. Time had lost its meaning. Weakness ached in her bones and made her flesh flabby as a caught fish turns soft in the air. But she had endured worse before, and she kept going. They would be somewhere on ahead, down the trail: Johnny, the sheep and the riders from Axe. They could be nowhere else.

She was confusedly aware that the heat of the sun had given way to coolness, the glare of light to thickening dusk. She would have to stop soon, would have to rest. Flesh could take only so much, either her own or that of her horse. It stumbled now and again as it moved.

She blinked and looked again, it was no mirage. That was not a low-hung star, but a fire—perhaps a cook fire on which fresh wood had been thrown. The red eye shone a long way in the night. As she glimpsed the beacon, she heard another sound, one strange and alien, but not to be mistaken—the steady, disturbed bleating of sheep.

Men were near the fire as she rode up, standing about in strained, unnatural attitudes. She had known that it would be this way; that was why she had come. She caught the glint of light on gun barrels, where some men watched others and held them like hounds on a leash.

A couple of men were dragging or carrying something, forcing their way among the sheep. She could make out the sheep, a vast gray mass in the uncertain gloom; the stars seemed more remote and aloof than she ever remembered seeing them.

The men had dropped whatever they were carrying and were pushing hastily back from among the sheep. Another was cursing, his voice shrill with anger and helpless rage. She caught enough of what he was mouthing to understand, and the night wind blew cold. Then a fist smashed against the speaker's mouth and silenced him.

It was Johnny they had lugged out there, Johnny, probably tied, certainly helpless. Now they were starting to yell, trying to run the sheep over him!

That much of their purpose was clear. Johnny Malcolm was to die beneath the hoofs of the sheep he'd brought to that land.

Myra cried wildly and drove her horse forward, and no one tried to stop her. The sheep were hesitant and uncertain, not quite ready to run. The shouting men fell silent as some of them recognized her. It was Myra M'Ginnis, or Vascom, and they were at a loss.

She reached Johnny and was off her horse and kneeling beside him, crying out, cradling his head in her arms, careless of the tar, shocked and enraged at sight of the feathers, as understanding came. She turned with a burst of anger which would have done credit to any of the Vascoms, as some of the men pressed closer.

Clayburn had been in charge of the night's work, doing Slade's bidding efficiently. He'd gotten a job on Axe a couple of years before, returning with Slade from one of the latter's periodical forays on a distant range. Discreetly, he had arrived alone, saying nothing about any acquaintance with the younger Vascom and, once hired, had demonstrated that he could do the work required.

Since that day he'd served Slade rather than Barney, having reason above and beyond the job for gratitude. But for Slade, he'd have lain forgotten in his grave for those two years. Slade had saved him from a hangrope which had already been adjusted about his neck. It had been a risk, even though Slade had had the drop, to free him. Thereafter they had ridden hard to evade a vengeful posse.

He scowled at Myra, his voice a harsh boom from deep in his throat.

'Sure we've tarred an' feathered him, ma'am. What should he expect, bringin' sheep to this range?'

'Sheep?' Myra cried. 'You're only using them as an excuse to mistreat a man you hate—a man who saved my life. And you're a cowardly bunch, so many of you jumping one man—'

'He had his own crew,' Clayburn reminded her uncomfortably. 'Only they were asleep on the job!'

'It amounted to the same thing, after you sneaked up on them! You must be proud of yourselves!'

Clayburn winced at the charge, as did some of the others. Coming from the lips of a beautiful woman, the indictment stung. Clayburn realized resentfully that Slade had left them to do the job and to take the full onus.

'Axe has had its way of doing for a long while, and I reckon it will keep right on,' Clayburn returned doggedly. 'And leavin' out the sheep, he's only getting what's coming to him. We've found out something that'll maybe interest you, ma'am. He murdered your husband, Leavitt Vascom—stuck a knife in him, then buried him, out by Lampases Spring!'

CHAPTER SEVENTEEN

Clayburn flung the accusation with calculated brutality. Report had it that this girl had been badly treated by Leavitt, coming very close to death. But Clayburn had seen how much she liked the fellow, and she had married him. Such news should overwhelm her, shut her up.

Myra heard the report without surprise. It came to her that she had expected something of the sort, really. Such an end for such a man was almost inevitable. It explained why nothing more had been heard of Leavitt recently, though he might have fled to another part of the country.

Far from being shocked, she was conscious of an overwhelming sense of relief, a lifting of the fear which had been with her against the time when he might return. As for what Johnny was being charged with—her breath caught as she saw how he had been mistreated.

She came defensively to her feet, faced them with head upflung. If this last year had been an ordeal by fire, she had come through it tempered and seasoned, with a beauty which until then had only been suggested.

'You're saying that Leavitt's dead,' she returned, 'even that he was killed. But all that you're doing is guessing, making wild charges to try and excuse yourself for something worse. If it's so, then he only got what was coming to him! He left me alone, to die, telling me to hurry up about it, because I was in his way! As for John Malcolm, I know this. He saved my life, and I'll stand by him. If you're going to murder him, you'll have to kill me first!'

Clayburn chewed his lip uneasily. His appeal to sympathy had backfired, even among his own men. Most of them knew Leavitt Vascom as well as he did, and they accepted her account, wasting no pity on him.

'You've done enough here,' Myra pressed her advantage. 'And what are you doing here in the first place? I don't believe Barney sent you on such a job. He never resorts to such sneaky methods of fighting. So you'd better go.'

Clayburn shrugged, eyeing his own crew, observing the building anger in the others. None of the riders of Axe were in a mood to continue the sport, and he knew uneasily that Myra was right, that the anger of Old Barney could be terrible. He turned and swung onto his horse, then rode away without a backward look.

The others let them go. Myra dropped on her knees beside Johnny, her eyes wide with pity.

'Build up the fire again and heat water,' she

commanded. 'Hurry. Oh, Johnny, Johnny, what have they done to you?'

★ ★ ★

Following her clash with Slade, Vivian moved restlessly, feeling increasingly trapped. Slade had overplayed his hand, lacking the patience which a true gambler should exercise, but he had made plain what he was after, and that she was the key by which he intended to obtain the big ranch. The thought was like a nightmare.

Even with him gone, the atmosphere of the house seemed heavy, oppressively surcharged. For he would be back. Worse, Barney was not returning.

The knowledge that Barney was not her father somehow did not surprise her. It left her with a feeling both of relief and pity for him, a greater understanding and sympathy than she had possessed before. The knowledge that he planned to pass over his own son and make her his heir was both surprising and frightening. For that intent had placed them both in jeopardy.

There could be a dozen explanations for Barney's continued absence, but she had a feeling that none were valid in this situation. Slade had made clear that he played a game for high stakes, in which both she and her father were mere pawns.

Whether or not she was Barney's child, she possessed his ability to reason coldly and logically. There was danger here. She would do better to get away while she could. And it would be well to ride armed.

There was always extra guns in Barney's room. She went to it, noting that the bed had been smoothed neatly, then left undisturbed. In a drawer of the desk she found a small but deadly derringer and slipped it into her dress.

Slade had said that Barney had ridden away. Apparently he had told the truth, since the house was empty. She was about to turn away when her eyes caught an alien speck near the middle of the floor.

There was no particular reason her pulse should falter, until a closer look confirmed her suspicion. The speck was a spot of dry blood, and there were other spots scattered across the room. Even in the fading light, she knew that she was not mistaken.

It was starting to grow dark outside, but the night seemed suddenly more friendly than the huge, silent house. Something had happened to Barney, and her imagination was far too lively in speculating on what it was.

The crew had returned, or at least many of them were coming in following the day's work. Light showed in cook house and bunk house alike. She considered questioning them, even asking for help, instituting a search for their employer. But she as quickly rejected the notion. Many, if not most of the men, were Slade's friends. Someone would be apt to carry tales to him. She must not spoil what chance there was.

She made her preparations calmly, working swiftly. She had to get to Wagon Wheel, and she prepared the baby for the ride, feeling a sharp twinge of regret. Its mother would be happy to have it again, but she would miss the baby. Still, she was its aunt, and this would not be a final parting.

That the outfit with which Axe had so long been feuding should offer sanctuary was not even ironical. One fact was clear. They were all in this together.

As she went out, she was surprised to see that the other buildings had gone dark. That was odd, since it was much too early for the men to go to bed. Usually they played cards and occupied themselves with small tasks for another hour or more.

The emptiness of barn and corrals confirmed a rising apprehension. The crew had gone off again, taking most of the riding animals. She found her own horse and saddled it. The night made a welcome shelter as she headed for Wagon Wheel.

It had been her plan to place the baby in Myra's arms, then to pour out her story to Howard Denning and ask his advice. But Lavinia Taylor gave her the disturbing news that Myra was gone. No one had any notion where.

As for Howard, he was asleep, worn out by worry and apprehension and the growing trouble of his own old injury.

'It'll be a mercy when John Malcolm gets back,' Lavinia declared. 'Howard's lost without him. And unless Ma gets better and comes back to look after Howard—my land, I don't know. The poor man is sick, and he needs better medicine than a doctor can give him!'

Under the circumstances, it would be cruel to disturb him, perhaps useless. Vivian thought regretfully of the bed she had counted on, then dismissed the temptation.

'There's something going on on this range,' she said. 'I don't know just what it is, but it means trouble. Can you look after the baby until Myra returns?'

'If I can't, I'm slipping,' Lavinia asserted. 'I've looked after more people, of just about any age or size you might mention, than I can count the years I've been around this country. And the one is all that makes the other worth thinking about.'

'I'm sure of that,' Vivian agreed. 'I'll have to be getting right back, but I know that you'll look after her.' In response to Lavinia's protest that she should not be riding at such an hour, her answer was simple, 'I must.'

Had Lavinia guessed that she was not returning to Axe and dared not, she would have been insistent. Swallowed again by the night, Vivian hesitated. Nagging fears were bad enough, but the worst part was that now she had to ride blindly, with only her instinct for guidance. Something was going on, but where or what she could only guess. Where would Slade have taken his father?

She swung north, with the stars for guidance, though she knew the country well enough to ride it blindfolded if need be. Her decision was based on what the men would call a hunch. Having chosen a course, she could only keep going, hoping and praying that she was right, and that she might not be too late.

The night wore itself away. Daylight was at once better and worse. The sun was friendly, but it could be pitilessly revealing, should enemies prowl these same wastes—and enemies might be riders from either outfit. She had brought no food, not having anticipated this additional journey. Hunger gnawed, and never had she felt so alone or friendless. The land lay wide and empty, beginning to burn under the sun of late June. Nowhere was there a cow or single stray, since the range had been swept clean.

The last time she had journeyed there had been with Johnny Malcolm. Remembering, her cheeks turned pink at the truancy of her thoughts. But there was no one to see or guess, and it was pleasant to lose herself in dreams.

She drank at the springs, and water was a big help. Having been raised in a saddle, she was making her way as straight as though guided by a compass. It was nearing mid-day when she glimpsed the cabin, and her breath quickened, half-fearfully, half-hopefully, at a sign of life: a thin trickle of smoke rising.

Since it was impossible to hide her approach, she put the horse to a run, and all at once it seemed that this must be an illusion; not the smoke, which was real and increasing, but the likelihood that it came from the chimney. The rusty snout of the stovepipe thrust above the roof exactly as it had done weeks before, but the smoke was coming from the opposite end of the cabin.

Apprehension gripped her, and she urged her tired horse to a still greater effort. Now it was clear enough, and she flung herself from the saddle, snatching at a large stick which lay nearby, tearing at the piled wood against the side of the shack. After smoking in uncertain fashion, it was just beginning to blaze vigorously. A moment more and the flame would have been beyond control. Tinder-dry as the old logs were, the cabin would have gone fast.

She saw something else as she tore at the piled wood, not only how carefully it had been arranged, with small sticks near the bottom and larger ones above; but also how dry grass had helped ignite the fire, a small fringe of partly burned grasses having dropped away. Still more revealing was the crotched stick and what it held, just ready to topple into the fire—the magnifying glass, its thick lens focusing the sun into a tiny red spot.

She had seen that glass many times in past years, and she recognized it with a mingled feeling of dismay and shame. Leavitt and Slade had treasured their fire maker. Once they had almost set the barn on fire in similar fashion.

There was a sound from inside the cabin. She hurried around to the door, finding it barred with a log brace on the outside. It was no surprise, once she had the door open, to see Barney seated uncertainly on the edge of the lower bunk.

CHAPTER EIGHTEEN

The column of smoke lifted and hung in the still air like a funeral pyre. Slade, viewing the beacon from a distance, smiled at the thought. That was what it was, and now it was too late to turn back. He had burned, if not his bridges, then his cabin, which in this case was more final.

It was too late even for regret, and he

sought impatiently to banish such shadows from his mind. After his discovery in the gulch above the cabin, he'd ridden hard, giving orders to Clayburn, despatching him with several of the crew. By this time those orders should have been executed, or be well on the way toward finality. They should, in fact, soon be returning, to report a mission accomplished.

So it was long past time for softness. If some parts of his program were tough, then it was because he'd been given no choice. When Barney had cut Leavitt and himself out of his will, he had in effect cut his own throat. He should have known that it was asking for trouble to leave Axe to Vivian.

The news had shocked Leavitt, too. Slade knew now that he'd had the same reaction, the same ambition: to marry Vivian, and thus possess the ranch. In Leavitt's case, the news had come at a most inopportune time, after he'd involved himself with Myra M'Ginnis.

Typically, Leavitt had set out to free himself of the encumbrance. That he had eliminated himself in the process was a stroke of luck.

What remained was to turn his back on that slowly fading column of smoke, and go ahead with other plans. He was Axe now, as the smoke testified, with no one strong enough to challenge what he did. Vivian could be handled, one way or another. All that remained was to gather up the loose threads, then weave them into one strand, under his control—

Slade scowled, disliking the simile; in his mind it suggested a rope, and a rope suggested a noose. Say rather, he'd pick up the pieces—

There was wind in the distance, wind which stirred small dust devils. But there was more than dust, gone into limbo. Something moved, momentarily glimpsed, lost again on the rim of the horizon. Unconsciously, Slade moved his tongue across lips gone suddenly dry and swung his horse, putting it to a run, heading in the opposite direction. Perhaps his imagination was playing tricks, and it was only dust; he hadn't been able to see too clearly. But no one should be riding off there, and he had to know.

After a mile, he slowed, going more carefully, like a man afraid—or a hunter stalking game. Brush and a few trees gave a clothed appearance to a gulch, and he followed along its bottom, almost to the crest of the slope where it began. Dismounting, he moved like an Indian.

From there he could see without being seen, and his breath caught in his throat. There was one horse, nearly a mile away, a single horse with two riders. Doubly burdened, it moved slowly, but as it approached he could see it clearly.

Barney Vascom was in the saddle, Vivian mounted behind him, her arms reaching forward on either side, steadying him as he rode. Far off to the north, the last smoke from the burning cabin was vanishing in the haze of summer.

Barney was far sicker than she'd counted on; by the time she had made sure of that, a tiny smoldering remnant of flame had taken fresh hold, and the old cabin had been too far gone to save.

Slade stared, his tongue nervously weaving patterns. Here was disaster. By some mischance, Vivian had gone to the cabin, reaching it in time to save Barney; but the evidence, even without what Barney could tell, was plain. The fire must have been burning when she arrived, already eating its way into the cabin.

Now he had really burned his bridges.

Before, he had had a hard choice to make, but it was as nothing compared to what confronted him now. Slade returned to his horse and reached for the rifle in the saddle sheath, fingering it reluctantly. Two quick, well-aimed bullets would be enough. After that, Axe would be his. For a will, even if it turned up, wouldn't matter, with Vivian and Leavitt both gone, and himself the sole remaining heir.

It had to be that way, for more than the ranch was at stake. His own neck was endangered, and the strands were making a noose in more ways than one.

The horse and its riders were closer as he returned to the crest, coming within range, yet far enough away so that they would not be able to sense anything wrong before he started shooting. Slade lifted the rifle, thrusting the butt of the stock hard against his shoulder, sighting along the barrel. His hands were clammy, and the front sight seemed to waver and blur.

He threw himself flat on the ground, resting the end of the barrel over a small stone. That was better. Both shots would have to be quick, before the horse could bolt, or any counter-action be taken. But to a man as skilled in marksmanship as he, there should be no problem. Slade closed one eye and curled a finger around the trigger.

Then he started and drew back, a curse rasping in his throat. Suddenly he was anxious to do the job, and now it was too late—though luck of a sort was with him, in that he hadn't pulled the trigger. Had he done so, the shots would have been widely heard, traced swiftly to him.

Off to the southeast, riders were coming into sight, men whose attitude indicated weariness. They had seen the single horse with its double burden and were heading to join Barney and Vivian. These were the men he'd despatched on a mission south, led by

Clayburn.

They should still have been many hours and hours away, but something had sent them hastening back far sooner than he'd expected. Whether the news they bore was good or bad no longer mattered. It was too late even for bullets, too late for everything.

No, perhaps not too late for one final act on his part. Seeing the others and the way they rode, Slade had a feeling that John Malcolm must still be alive, still moving the sheep toward Wagon Wheel. One thing remained: to settle with Johnny.

CHAPTER NINETEEN

Blood dripped from the spear-tipped points of Slade's spurs and stained his horse's sides in ragged streaks. It was an outward indication of the raging frustration which he could no longer keep bottled. He pulled up in the shelter of a draw which was close enough so that, with luck, he might be able to hear what was said as the crew joined Vivian and Barney. Amazement and concern were in their voices as they greeted Barney, asking what had happened.

Barney grunted, not choosing to enlighten them. He was in a dour mood, still far from shaking off the effects of the blow which had come close to cracking his skull. His speech was thick and uncertain, but Vivian knew better than to try to take charge at such a moment.

'Never mind me,' he growled. 'The question is, where have you fellows been—and what've you been doing? And who gave you leave?'

Clayburn reluctantly undertook to answer.

'We rode a day's journey south,' he explained. 'Slade told us what to do, said he was relayin' your orders, so of course we followed them.'

That wasn't quite true. Slade had made it clear that the others of the crew should assume that the orders came from Barney, but Clayburn had known better.

It sounded plausible enough, under the circumstances. Barney's tongue thickened.

'What did he tell you to do?'

'He said you wanted the sheep met—and stopped.'

Barney was conscious of the sudden tightening embrace of Vivian's arms. He was equally aware of the increasing pain in his skull, as though the broken blade of the Axe had crashed there. Stubbornly, he gave no sign.

'And what did you do? You got a tongue to talk with?'

'We sent word ahead by Leseur that they'd come far enough. When they didn't pay attention, we stopped them. Got the jump on them.'

'Mister—' the use of such a title, even without the brittleness of the tone, was warning to any who knew Barney—'my patience is frayin' like a worn-out lasso. *What'd you do?*'

Clayburn shrugged. If the old man wanted it, he could have it.

'We gave Malcolm the tar and feather treatment.' Again, Barney felt the convulsive clasp of the arms about his waist. 'If he's fool enough still to try and keep coming after that—'

'Tar and feathers, eh?' Barney's tone lost its rasp, became almost conversational. 'And I suppose he let you?'

'It took some doing,' Clayburn conceded, 'but we had the men.'

'And the jump, like you said,' Barney supplied dryly. 'You make me proud to be the boss of Axe—of such a stinkin', cowardly bunch, that a coyote would turn up his nose at! You're fired, Clayburn. You've worked to double-cross me ever since I took you on, at Slade's recommendation. So from now on you can draw your pay from him—a pair of rattlesnakes! I—'

His voice rasped again, broke, and Barney slumped forward in the saddle. But for Vivian's clasp he would have fallen. Saliva drooled from the corner of his mouth, suddenly slack.

By the time the confusion ended and the silent, chastened group were on their way to the buildings, one thing was clear. Barney, if not already dead, was dying. Slade watched impersonally. He might still be able to take control.

Clayburn was prudently withdrawing, following Barney's final ultimatum. As soon as he could manage it without being seen, Slade took out after him. Clayburn was riding fast.

Slade was impatient for the rest of the story concerning Malcolm, the details of which had not been supplied. Tar and feathers alone could be a light punishment. But if the victim resisted and was severely manhandled, a man might not survive.

Once or twice Slade shouted, but the distance was too great. Clayburn rode without looking back. Press his horse as he would, Slade was slow in narrowing the gap.

He was heading into rough, broken country. Slade took a short cut, and Clayburn was lost to sight. Then the sound of voices, from close at hand, brought him up short. The one belonged to Clayburn. The other belonged to the bounty hunter, and it came as chill as December wind.

'Take it easy, mister.' Wardlaw's voice was a drawl, but its authority suggested that he might be looking at the other man along the barrel of a gun. 'I'd like a word with you—maybe two or three.'

'Sure, as many as you like.' Clayburn was cool in a pinch. 'But you don't need that gun.'

'We'll keep it, just the same. You see, I'm trainin' this Colt to be a wild horse. And it runs in my mind that I ought to know you, as though I'd seen you before. Or could it be that I've studied your likeness on a dodger?'

'Not likely. I'm Clayburn, foreman for Axe. This is Axe range you're on.'

'Now I know you're a liar,' the bounty hunter returned pleasantly. 'Barney Vascom rods his own spread. And Clayburn ain't the moniker I've seen along with your likeness. But right now I'm not interested in you—all I want is some information.'

'Fair enough. Only you've confused me with somebody else.'

'I don't make mistakes. Can't afford to in my business. But you're small potatoes,' Wardlaw added contemptuously. 'There's only a hundred measly bucks reward for you, and I don't fish for minnows. You just had a meeting with your boss; then the rest of them went one way and you another. Why?'

'Barney seemed to have some sort of a stroke. He'd worked himself all up—firin' me. I figure he was really mad at his son Slade, who'd given me my orders. He claimed that they hadn't come from him.'

'A stroke? You figure Barney's about to cash in?'

'Not likely.' Clayburn was contemptuous. 'He's tough.'

Slade understood Wardlaw's interest. His own ability to pay the promised bribe might hinge on that point.

'You say he was peevish at Slade. Just what did he say?'

'Plenty. Sounded like he was just getting warmed up when that fit took him. As it was, he called Slade a rattlesnake. Reckon he'll be just about that popular around this range from now on.'

Slade cursed under his breath at the man's volubility. That word was damning, and no one knew it better than the bounty hunter. For a wild moment, Slade thought of shooting Wardlaw in the back before he suspected danger. But the crew might still be within sound of gunfire; it could be too risky.

Wardlaw had lost interest. 'Better keep riding, like Barney told you,' he instructed. 'Just one thing. Don't try to find Slade, or side him. If you did that, I might find you worth enough—dead—to take you in, along with him.'

'Don't worry.' Clayburn shrugged. 'I ain't so big a fool as to risk my neck for such as him.'

Clayburn's estimate of Barney's toughness had been in error. The boss of Broken Axe was dead, and the world, none too cheerful at any time, seemed doubly desolate. Rain, coming when no one had expected it, added to the appearance of gloom. It was as though nature wept for the man who had inspired few tears while living.

Vivian was genuinely sorry. If anything, she was more grief-stricken than could have been the case if she had still believed him her father. Somehow the recent revelations made everything both better and worse, showing him to be the lonely man he had been. Of her own changed status because of these developments, she had no time to think.

Myra arrived in the midst of the confusion, bringing sympathy and news at once disturbing and startling. She was able to add details to what Clayburn had said about Johnny Malcolm and the sheep and the manner in which he had been treated. Vivian's eagerness for news was unmistakable, and Myra smiled at her through a mist of tears.

'That's the main reason why I hurried back and came to see you first thing,' she explained. 'Johnny's all right. But for a while he was so done in that he was delirious. While he was that way, he kept saying your name, Vivian—calling for you. I thought you'd want to know.'

'Oh, I do,' Vivian breathed. 'It's wonderful of you to tell me.'

Myra was understanding and sympathetic, gravely honest.

'He saved my life, and I think perhaps I may have saved his,' she said. 'That makes me feel better. I'll admit that since I've had my eyes opened—well, I've come to appreciate Johnny more than I did a year ago. And if things had been different—but at least I've some memories, and the baby, thanks to both of you for taking care of her. And it's you he loves, Vivian. I'm not going to give any advice, but I wouldn't let a man like that go—or find out that I owned a big ranch before he'd had time to tell me other things. For he's proud. And another reason why I wouldn't waste any time—I'd want to make sure that he got this far alive!'

Action had always been a characteristic of Barney Vascom. In that moment Vivian was definitely a Vascom.

'Thank you for everything, Myra,' she agreed. 'I've had my eyes opened, too, lately. I won't waste any time.'

The unexpected storm caught Slade by surprise, drenching him, adding to the savagery of his mood. He found temporary shelter, then, as the rain settled to a lasting downpour, realized that he could not wait it out. It had become vital that he finish his own chores; he had to succeed where others had failed. If he could settle with Malcolm, there would be no one to stand long in the way of his control of this range. Under those circumstances, the bounty hunter could be dealt with—one way or another.

There was one good thing about the storm. He'd be less visible or open to discovery by Wardlaw as he rode. His horse had been grazing, finding the wet grass to its taste. He tightened the cinch, then, swinging to the saddle, glimpsed another rider, briefly revealed, then shrouded again by the storm.

Quivering, the cayuse poised an instant, then jumped to the rake of the spurs. Slade's mind, spurred by jealousy, fitted the pieces together. Either Barney was already dead, or desperately sick. Why else would Vivian set out at such a time, heading south—where Johnny was? It was only too plain to his inflamed mind.

The storm seemed to thicken, the rain continuing hour after hour. A couple of times, when the downpour slackened, he caught sight of Vivian well ahead. Try as he might, he could not narrow the gap.

Early darkness crept across the land as he neared the Termagent, running high and muddy. The sheep should be just about that far along, but at least they were still on the far side. This might be a good place to wait. Slade sought shelter, heading for the abandoned cabin of the former ferryman, a shack set somewhat back from the river, hidden among a clump of trees.

It had a musty smell, having been unused for more than a year. Rats and mice had made themselves at home, but at least the place was dry. Slade looked about hopefully for food, on the chance that some tinned goods might have been left behind. A loose plank in the floor responded to his efforts, and momentarily he believed that he had found such a cache.

There was a can, stowed where dirt had been excavated to make room. Then he saw that the can was too big for fruit or vegetables, and he scowled in disgust as he made out what it was—a sealed keg of black blasting powder. The ferryman had probably kept it on hand to knock loose drifting trees or logs, when they lodged at dangerous spots in the ferryboat's channel.

Apparently the keg had been left behind when the bridge was built. Since it was sealed, the powder should be as good as ever. A gleam came to Slade's eyes.

Near the can was a length of fuse. There was still perhaps half an hour of daylight, enough for his purpose. And the sheep were still somewhere on the far side of the river.

Carrying the keg, Slade walked to the bridge, then ducked beneath it. The Termagent was running high, showing the effects of the steady downpour, which was probably worse farther upstream. It had risen nearly a foot, creeping under the bridge so that there was barely room to place the keg and its fuse.

Lighting it, Slade followed the sheltering fringe of brush back to the cabin. There he waited.

The blast should come at any instant. He found a better vantage point and gasped, then broke into a run, shouting hoarsely. But even as desperation assailed him, he knew that he'd be too late.

While he'd moved back out of sight, a horseman had come along the road and was now near the middle of the bridge. Vivian. He'd supposed that she was well ahead, long past that point. Even as he yelled, the rending boom of the giant powder smothered the sound.

CHAPTER TWENTY

Myra had not overstated the situation. John Malcolm had been badly spent after the tar and feathers and the beating. But Myra had come, like an angel of mercy, taking charge, soothing and restoring him in more ways than with food and warmth. Looking back the next morning, after his friends had cleaned him up and he'd fallen asleep, he had some uneasy moments. He'd been delirious, and he wasn't at all sure that he'd not mistaken Myra for Vivian, or what tricks his tongue might have played under those conditions.

But if so, Myra had been understanding and cheerfully friendly when she had set out on her return journey. She had parried his appreciation with a smile and a slightly shaky laugh.

'You saved *my* life, Johnny,' she reminded him. 'So now we're fairly even. Better late than never, they say.' Not explaining that, she ended with a rush, 'Being able to do something makes me feel as though I have some reason for being alive.'

As he went on with the sheep, it was apparent that she had encountered others and spread a new gospel among them. Everywhere was a new and friendlier atmosphere.

After she had gone, Johnny remembered that first moment, when Clayburn had made his charges concerning Leavitt. She had asked no questions. Clearly she had disdained to. It was reassuring to know that such friends remained.

The unseasonable storm surprised them as much as anyone. The sheep did not seem to mind, but the men, riding soaked, were less appreciative.

'Sure the rain 'll do the range a lot of good,' Cy Robbins conceded. 'Couldn't be better for the country. But me, I ain't a duck, and I can't help but ponder some questions. One is, is any of this rain fallin' up on Wagon Wheel, where we really need it? And why should *I* get so much? I don't rightly figure to require so much bathin'.'

'Maybe nature knows best. Or maybe it's just confused your smell with the sheep, not findin' no diff'rence,' a companion suggested.

So prolonged a storm was unusual for so late in the season. The ground become almost a morass. They ate cold meals and slept in damp blankets. Even the sheep looked sodden.

It was late when they sighted the river. Even from a distance, it appeared high and muddy, boiling along as though angry at itself and eager to reach a milder land.

'She's a shrew for sure,' Robbins observed. 'Lucky we ain't got to face her raw, the way they used to before the bridge was built.'

'Or back before the ferry,' an old-timer put it. 'She used to separate the men from the boys in those days. The good died young—and sudden.'

Fresh thunder jarred the closing dusk. The bridge, just coming into sight, reared like a bucking horse. A giant cotton boll seemed to burst open at its far end. Then the bridge settled back, churning the river to a wilder frenzy.

The current slashed at the sudden barricade, wrenching in a frenzy. What was left of the far side of the bridge swung majestically. The nearer end, still anchored to the shore, yielded to the strain. There was a crack of timbers as it tore; then the bridge was gone, a plaything of the river.

That part Johnny observed without conscious effort. His attention was focused on the horse and rider who had been in the middle of the bridge when it went into convulsions. The horse raced desperately and was almost at the shore when its footing gave way, spilling cayuse and rider like straws.

At that point the road twisted downstream, so that the action was above him. And on that southern bank, the land stretched wide and easy, by contrast with the formidably rearing cliffs which circumscribed it on the north shore.

Johnny pushed his horse into the current, scanning it hopefully. Darkness was pushing a blanket over land and water, and the trangled mass of debris which had been the bridge made it worse. Then he made out something which no longer struggled, swept along by the current. The horse had been fatally hurt as it hit the water.

He had his lariat loose and ready, though no longer even daring to hope. Then he glimpsed the whiteness of an arm, as if in a beckoning gesture. He shouted and flung the loop, and drew it back as the hungry current fought against giving up its prey. Only as she was drawn alongside did he know surely that it was Vivian.

He pulled her up onto his horse, and her arms crept about his neck and clung.

'Johnny!' she sobbed. 'Hold me close! Don't ever let me go!'

Slade made out the scene, dim in the distance, the rain and dusk. He lifted his rifle, his face twisting, but lowered it again. His hands were shaking too much for a shot, and this had to be sure.

Beyond a few bruises, Vivian had not been hurt. Her horse had acted as a buffer when they struck the water, flinging her clear. After making sure of that, Johnny headed toward the camp, which was already being set up.

The news she brought was both good and bad. Barney Vascom was dead, and the personal significance of that did not occur to Johnny for some time. He had made clear to Vivian, on the journey from the burning cabin, that his rage was not against the sheep or even Wagon Wheel. Now a reaction was setting in across the range. While the sheep would not be welcomed, they would be accepted.

If they could be gotten that far. That was the next question, with the bridge out. Even cattle, in the old days, had been forced into a week-long detour around that portion of the Termagent. Establishment of the ferry had saved many days, though crossing on it was a slow and sometimes hazardous job. The bridge had made a big difference.

Vivian had another piece of news. Ma Denning had sent word that the latest operation had been a success. It wouldn't be too long before she'd be coming home, to look after Howard and the rest of her boys.

The news about Barney decided Johnny. A week would be too long to go around by the ford, for then they'd miss Barney's funeral. And a man should have at least one of his kin and some of his friends to mourn him.

'Maybe we can use the ferry,' Johnny said. 'We'll have a try. If it works, they can shuttle the sheep across as well. It ought to work.'

Morning brought an end to the rain, though the clouds still clustered as though reluctant to desert the river. Johnny examined the ferryboat, still tied in a sheltered cove on their shore, the long, heavy rope running from it up to the steel cable which spanned the stream. On the far side, where the cliffs rose inhospitably, a sort of dock had been built, part way up the portal, with a road leading back. The ferry was sometimes even with the dock, sometimes a foot or so above or below, depending on the height of the river. But it had been a big improvement, prior to the bridge.

The ferryman, who had operated the big raft for more than a score of years, had left the country when the bridge had been opened. Oley had opined that his job was done, and decided to warm his old bones in the Arizona sun.

Without his skill, it wouldn't be simple to operate the ferry, but it should be possible. The process was relatively simple. Loaded and eased from its harbor into the current, the raft bobbed cork-like at the end of its pulley and heavy rope, while the cable stretched. Those on board pulled it along, hand over hand, by another double rope, stretched from shore to shore, and still in place. The method was primitive, but it worked. Johnny had crossed there more than once.

Normally, it was a ten-minute passage either way. One man, with the strength possessed by Oley, could manage the empty ferry. Two or three could tug it along with a load. By some trick of the river, the current helped more than it hindered.

Johnny was for making the first crossing with a couple of men, to make sure that it could be done. Vivian vetoed that.

'I'm going with you. If anything happens, I want to be with you. I think I've earned that right, Johnny.'

There could be no question of that. And whether the hazard would be greater or less, there was no sure way of telling. Unless Slade had become a madman—

They tied two horses on board, to ride on toward Wheel and Axe. The raft could be pulled back, with him at the rope on the far side, if they made it all right. They cast off, and the raft wobbled and weaved crazily as the current caught it and the cable stretched. The first part was easy, the river aiding, others pulling at the rope on the south bank.

Then, past the middle, it became grueling work, with the crosscable stretched taut like an inverted V, the river angry about them. Now it was hand over hand to win their way forward, a painful inching along. Vivian was helping, smiling as she pulled.

They were almost to the dock when a shot sounded, and the rope went slack in their grasp. The ferry jerked wildly, bobbing loosely.

The pull rope had been cut by a bullet. It was Slade's answer. Not daring to come down to the dock and cut it with a knife, where he would be in sight and easily targeted, he had kept out of sight on the cliffs above, timing his shot as he chose.

He had not put his bullet into Johnny, but what might yet happen was not pleasant to think about. It had suddenly become a cat and mouse game. The raft was already partly crippled, and Slade could stalk them from the shelter of the high cliff, keeping out of sight, venting his vengeance in whatever way appealed to him.

A second, more violent jerk showed that he intended to go all the way, though by indirect methods. The steel cable, holding the heavy rope which anchored the ferry, snapped loose and writhed wildly above the river.

Unlike the pull rope, the cable was anchored higher up and farther back, out of sight. It had been twisted twice around a tree and tied. There, unhindered, Slade had worked to loosen it, releasing it at a picked instant. Now there was nothing to hold them.

The pulley screamed along the steel strand and tore loose, and the raft plunged, rudderless in the grip of the current, heading straight into white water. Not far below, the stream narrowed, thundering through a gorge between high walls. Then, a mile farther downstream, it plunged in wild abandon over a deep waterfall.

CHAPTER TWENTY-ONE

The raft lurched, twisting, then straightened and surged ahead. The horses were mad with terror. One of them leaped over the rail, then was brought up, threshing wildly, by its halter rope. It was on the lower side of the craft, and the current sucked it under and held it. The impediment seemed to make little difference in the force which the river exerted.

Free from the anchoring cable, there was

no power which could stop or even slow the raft, short of the plunge which would splinter it into wreckage. There was no pole or sweep to steer with, and even had there been, there was no beach, as had been the case a short time before, no place to land. Now the gorge enclosed them, walls of rock rearing on either side. The hemmed waters slashed back in fury at such confinement.

Vivian's face had gone white, more from watching the horse than from their own peril. Slade's action was clear enough to both. Once they were gone, there would be no one between him and control of Broken Axe. An extra killing or so made no particular difference to a man already in the shadow of the noose.

Vivian looked at Johnny, and there was sweetness in the set of her lips, the willingness to face even this along with him. His throat felt tight. But he was not ready to accept defeat. There was a chance, however slim. He snatched at the rope at which they had been pulling only moments before. He'd prided himself on his handiness with a rope; now was the time to put it to use.

Only partly understanding, Vivian watched as he built a loop in the end of the rope—an end showing ragged and torn. At least the rope was stout, barely rotted by the year of inactivity since the bridge had replaced the ferry. It should be good for any test to which it was subjected, and there was plenty of rope. After breaking, the loose part had whipped loose from the tree and pulley on the south bank, and part still trailed in the water.

'Be ready to take a snub around the post,' he instructed, 'if I make a catch.' The post was a stout section of log, solidly anchored at one end of the raft. It had served to fasten the ferry when not in use.

Vivian nodded understandingly, pulling in some of the rope and coiling it, holding it so as to afford him such slack as might be needed. Johnny poised, looking up at the high cliff above. They were close to the northern rim, swept over by the current. The top of the cliff was a score of feet overhead.

This would require luck to begin with, as well as skill. The unhampered ferryboat was moving fast, but that was not too great a cause for worry. He'd roped moving targets many times from the back of a running horse, and this was roughly comparable. The rub now was that he'd never traveled through this canyon—nor had any other man made the journey and lived to report.

So he didn't know on what to depend. But if there should be some outjutting of rock near the top of the cliff, or a possible tree branch, anything which would serve as a target and might give reasonably solid anchorage, there would be a chance. He saw what he'd hoped for even as he finished making a noose, and loosed the loop in a swift upward fling.

It was tricky roping, in that, while the target was standing still, it was overhead instead of on the level; and he'd have only one try. Tension was in him, and he seemed to jerk in sympathy as he felt the noose catch. 'Now!' he yelled, and Vivian responded with the skilled speed of a trained roper. She whipped a double loop of the rope around the post, snubbing it, and braced desperately.

The jerk on the rope from above almost lifted Johnny from his feet, but almost instantly the strain was transferred to the rope and post as the line went taut. The raft spun in a wild gyration, and the remaining horse was flung over the side and under. Vivian was on her knees, still holding grimly. Johnny jumped to aid her, pulling in more of the slack, tying it fast.

The prisoned raft was in a bad spot, spray washing over it, drenching them with each raging sweep of the current. But at least the headlong race toward disaster had been checked. There was still a nagging worry that this might be temporary, however. Should the jutting thumb of rock crack, or prove less solid than it looked, they'd be on their way again; the rope might break in the savage tug of war with the current, or the old post rip loose.

The rope was stretched at a long taut angle,

the raft making it twirl and dance. He guessed that they had come half the distance toward the waterfall. To swim was out of the question.

The loop had caught the outcrop about a yard below the top of the ledge. High enough, with luck. He fumbled for his pocket knife and cut off the extra rope, handing it to Vivian.

'Tie one end about your waist,' he instructed, and fastened the other around his own. 'I'll climb to the top. When I'm up, then you come.'

She nodded comprehendingly, but her eyes closed tightly at the hazard of the web-thin, nervously twitching rope. Blindly she was in his arms, her hands eager, her lips salty. After a moment she pushed him back, managing a smile.

'You'll make it, Johnny,' she said, and the declaration was like a promise.

The rope was like a wildly plucked fiddle string, swinging and jerking to the bobbing of the raft. To climb straight up would have been easier, but he had to make his way along it at an angle.

The soaked strands were harsh, but he inched along; then the outcrop was ahead, above. He got a grip on an upper edge and lifted himself, preparatory to the final effort of pulling himself onto solid ground—and looked into the mocking face of Slade

Vascom.

The shock was unnerving. It hadn't occurred to him that Slade would ride along the rim, to follow the progress of the cast-off raft and check so carefully on his vengeance. Save for the knife scar, like a red dimple, on Slade's cheek, it was as though he again stared into the face of Leavitt, knife in hand.

There were no fingers on his throat, and there was water below, instead of rock grinding into his back, but in such a current he would be like driftwood. And there was a knife in Slade's hand as he reached to slash the rope.

It was a tortured face, but Slade had gone too far to draw back. He swept downward with the knife, leaning, and Johnny risked his precarious grip and grabbed, closing his fingers on the knife wrist. The blade twisted, scarring his own wrist, a sharp prick which had a good effect. It enraged Johnny, lending him strength. He twisted and dragged downward, and the scar stood out more vividly against a paling cheek. The knife slipped and was gone.

Johnny still held his grip, and terror outran the pain in the eyes of the trapped man. He tried to pull back, and slipped.

A greater weight jerked at Johnny's arms, almost more than he could bear. Slade had gone over in a sudden tumbling scramble. One of Johnny's hands clasped the rope, close to the rock anchor, a far from sure grip, but one into which he put all his might. He was leaning crazily, his other hand still holding Slade's wrist, keeping him from making the plunge.

He wrenched air back into straining lungs, wondering if he could manage. Neither of his hands could hold out very long. But if they forgot their differences long enough to work together, they might get out of this alive. And Slade possessed the same ambition, the same hate and terror and wish to live.

He was about to suggest the idea to Slade, to explain what he would need to do. But Slade writhed upward with a frantic twist, and his teeth tore at Johnny's clasping fingers. It was too much.

The relief from strain as he lost his hold was enough to enable him to reach and get a fresh grip on the outcrop of stone. He clung for a minute, resting, then pulled himself up and flopped on the ground. Again he lay a while, then turned, reassured by the tautness of the rope about his waist. Vivian's face seemed small and white amid the spray on the still tossing raft. He waved, and she climbed to him, with his help.

The sun broke through the clouds as she stood beside him. Slade's horse cropped the grass not far away.

From the landing, they waved in signal to the crew on the other shore. They would have to take the long drive around, but that no longer made much difference. It wouldn't be too far to a place where they could find another horse. Not that Johnny minded riding double, with Vivian in front in his arms. Even the horse seemed to find it a good arrangement.

On their ride north, Vivian confided one fact which was a fitting epitaph for Barney.

'He thought that sheep might be a good idea for this range,' she explained. 'He said that if they were run right, with plenty of pasture, so that the grass wasn't eaten too short—it should be the answer to a lot of problems. And he pointed out that Axe and Wheel together would make just such a spread. He wanted peace and prosperity; not trouble.'

'We'll work it out,' Johnny promised. 'And I like that word: together.'